PAPL
DISCARDED

Rumpole Rests His Case

John Mortimer

Rumpole Rests His Case

viking

VIKING
Published by the Penguin Group
Penguin Putnam Inc., 375 Hudson Street,
New York, New York 10014, U.S.A.
Penguin Books Ltd, 80 Strand,
London WC2R 0RL, England
Penguin Books Australia Ltd, 250 Camberwell Road, Camberwell,
Victoria 3124, Australia
Penguin Books Canada Ltd, 10 Alcorn Avenue,
Toronto, Ontario, Canada M4V 3B2
Penguin Books India (P) Ltd, 11 Community Centre, Panchsheel Park,
New Delhi – 110 017, India
Penguin Books (N.Z.) Ltd, Cnr Rosedale and Airborne Roads, Albany,
Auckland, New Zealand
Penguin Books (South Africa) (Pty) Ltd, 24 Sturdee Avenue,
Rosebank, Johannesburg 2196, South Africa

Penguin Books Ltd, Registered Offices:
Harmondsworth, Middlesex, England

First published in 2002 by Viking Penguin,
a member of Penguin Putnam Inc.

1 3 5 7 9 10 8 6 4 2

Copyright © Advanpress Ltd, 2001
All rights reserved

Grateful acknowledgment is made for permission to reprint an excerpt from "Leda and the
Swan" from *The Collected Works of W. B. Yeats: Volume I*, revised, edited by Richard J.
Finneran. Copyright © 1928 by The Macmillan Company, copyright renewed 1956 by
Georgie Yeats. Reprinted with permission of Scribner, an imprint of Simon & Schuster Adult
Publishing Group.

Publisher's Note
This is a work of fiction. Names, characters, places, and incidents either are the product of
the author's imagination or are used fictitiously, and any resemblance to actual persons, living or dead, business establishments, events, or locales is entirely coincidental.

LIBRARY OF CONGRESS CATALOGING-IN-PUBLICATION DATA

Mortimer, John Clifford, 1923–
Rumpole rests his case / John Mortimer.
p. cm.
ISBN 0-670-03139-9
1. Rumpole, Horace (Fictitious character)—Fiction. 2. Detective and mystery stories, English.
3. London (England)—Fiction. 4. Legal stories, English. I. Title.
PR6025.07552 R83 2002
823'.914—dc21 2002019046

This book is printed on acid-free paper. ∞

Printed in the United States of America
Set in Monotype Plantin

Without limiting the rights under copyright reserved above, no part of this publication
may be reproduced, stored in or introduced into a retrieval system, or transmitted, in any form
or by any means (electronic, mechanical, photocopying, recording or otherwise), without the
prior written permission of both the copyright owner and the above publisher of this book.

For Ann Mallalieu and Tim Cassel

Contents

Rumpole Rests His Case

Rumpole and the Old Familiar Faces

In the varied ups and downs, the thrills and spills in the life of an Old Bailey hack, one thing stands as stone. Your ex-customers will never want to see you again. Even if you've steered them through the rocks of the prosecution case and brought them out to the calm waters of a not-guilty verdict, they won't plan further meetings, host reunion dinners or even send you a card on your birthday. If they catch a glimpse of you on the Underground, or across a crowded wine bar, they will bury their faces in their newspapers or look studiously in the opposite direction.

This is understandable. Days in Court probably represent a period of time they'd rather forget and, as a rule, I'm not especially keen to renew an old acquaintance when a face I once saw in the Old Bailey Dock reappears at a 'Scales of Justice' dinner or the Inns of Court garden party. Reminiscences of the past are best avoided and what is required is a quick look and a quiet turn away. There have been times, however, when recognizing a face seen in trouble has greatly assisted me in the solution of some legal problem, and carried me to triumph in a difficult case. Such occasions have been rare, but like number thirteen buses, two of them turned up in short order round a Christmas which I remember as being one of the oddest, but certainly the most rewarding, I ever spent.

'A traditional British pantomime. There's nothing to beat it!'

'You go to the pantomime, Rumpole?' Claude Erskine-Brown asked with unexpected interest.

'I did when I was a boy. It made a lasting impression on me.'

'Pantomime?' The American Judge who was our fellow guest round the Erskine-Brown dinner table was clearly a stranger to such delights. 'Is that some kind of mime show? Lot of feeling imaginary walls and no one saying anything?'

'Not at all. You take some good old story, like Robin Hood.'

'Robin Hood's the star?'

'Well, yes. He's played by some strapping girl who slaps her thighs and says lines like "Cheer up, Babes in the Wood, Robin's not far away".'

'You mean there's cross-dressing?' The American visitor was puzzled.

'Well, if you want to call it that. And Robin's mother is played by a red-nosed comic.'

'A female comic?'

'No. A male one.'

'It sounds sexually interesting. We have clubs for that sort of thing in Pittsburgh.'

'There's nothing sexual about it,' I assured him. 'The dame's a comic character who gets the audience singing.'

'Singing?'

'The words come down on a sort of giant song-sheet,' I explained. 'And she, who is really a he, gets the audience to sing along.'

Emboldened by Erskine-Brown's claret (smoother on the

tongue but with less of a kick than Château Thames Embankment), I broke into a stanza of the song I was introduced to by Robin Hood's masculine mother.

> 'I may be just a nipper,
> But I've always loved a kipper . . .
> And so does my loving wife.
> If you've got a girl just slip her
> A loving golden kipper
> And she'll be yours for life.'

'Is that all?' The transatlantic Judge still seemed puzzled.

'All I can remember.'

'I think you're wrong, Mr Rumpole.'

'What?'

'I think you're wrong and those lines do indeed have some sexual significance.' And the Judge fell silent, contemplating the unusual acts suggested.

'I see they're doing *Aladdin* at the Tufnell Park Empire. Do you think the twins might enjoy it, Rumpole?'

The speaker was Mrs Justice Erskine-Brown (Phillida Trant as she was in happier days when I called her the Portia of our Chambers), still possessed of a beauty that would break the hearts of the toughest prosecutors and make old lags swoon with lust even as she passed a stiff custodial sentence. The twins she spoke of were Tristan and Isolde, so named by her opera-loving husband Claude, who was now bending Hilda's ear on the subject of Covent Garden's latest *Ring* cycle.

'I think the twins would adore it. Just the thing to cure the Wagnerian death-wish and bring them into a world of sanity.'

'Sanity?' The visiting Judge sounded doubtful. 'With old guys dressed up as mothers?'

'I promise you, they'll love every minute of it.' And then I made another promise that sounded rash even as I spoke the words. 'I know I would. I'll take them myself.'

'Thank you, Rumpole.' Phillida spoke in her gentlest judicial voice, but I knew my fate was sealed. 'We'll keep you to that.'

'It'll have to be after Christmas,' Hilda said. 'We've been invited up to Norfolk for the holiday.'

As she said the word 'Norfolk', a cold, sneeping wind seemed to cut through the central heating of the Erskine-Browns' Islington dining-room and I felt a warning shiver.

I have no rooted objection to Christmas Day, but I must say it's an occasion when time tends to hang particularly heavily on the hands. From the early-morning alarm call of carols piping on Radio Four to the closing headlines and a restless, liverish sleep, the day can seem as long as a fraud on the Post Office tried before Mr Injustice Graves.

It takes less than no time for me to unwrap the tie which I will seldom wear, and for Hilda to receive the annual bottle of lavender water which she lays down rather than puts to immediate use. The highlights after that are the Queen's speech, when I lay bets with myself as to whether Hilda will stand to attention when the television plays the National Anthem, and the thawed-out Safeway's bird followed by port (an annual gift from my faithful solicitor, Bonny Bernard) and pudding. I suppose what I have against Christmas Day is that the Courts are all shut and no one is being tried for anything.

That Christmas, Hilda had decided on a complete change of routine. She announced it in a circuitous fashion by saying, one late November evening, 'I was at school with Poppy Longstaff.'

'What's that got to do with it?' I knew the answer to this question, of course. Hilda's old school has this in common with polar expeditions, natural disasters and the last war: those who have lived through it are bound together for life and can always call on each other for mutual assistance.

'Poppy's Eric is Rector of Coldsands. And for some reason or other he seems to want to meet you, Rumpole.'

'Meet me?'

'That's what she said.'

'So does that mean I have to spend Christmas in the Arctic Circle and miss our festivities?'

'It's not the Arctic Circle. It's Norfolk, Rumpole. And our festivities aren't all that festive. So, yes. You have to go.' It was a judgment from which there was no possible appeal.

My first impression of Coldsands was of a gaunt church tower, presumably of great age, pointing an accusing finger to heaven from a cluster of houses on the edge of a sullen, gun-metal sea. My second was one of intense cold. As soon as we got out of the taxi, we were slapped around the face by a wind which must have started in freezing Siberia and gained nothing in the way of warmth on its journey across the plains of Europe.

'In the bleak mid-winter/ Frosty winds made moan . . .' wrote that sad old darling, Christina Rossetti. Frosty winds had made considerable moan round the Rectory at Coldsands, owing to the doors that stopped about an inch short of the stone floors and the windows which never shut properly, causing the curtains to billow like the sails of a ship at sea.

We were greeted cheerfully by Poppy. Hilda's friend had one of those round, childishly pretty faces often seen on seriously fat women, and she seemed to keep going on incessant cups of hot, sweet tea and a number of cardigans. If she moved like an enormous tent, her husband Eric was a slender wraith of a man with a high aquiline nose, two flapping wings of grey hair on the sides of his face and a vague air of perpetual anxiety, broken now and then by high and unexpected laughter. He made cruciform gestures, as though remembering the rubric 'Spectacles, testicles, wallet and watch' and forgetting where these important articles were kept.

'Eric,' his wife explained, 'is having terrible trouble with the church tower.'

'Oh dear.' Hilda shot me a look of stern disapproval, which I knew meant that it would be more polite if I abandoned my overcoat while tea was being served. 'How worrying for you, Eric.'

The Rev. Eric went into a long, excited and high-pitched speech. The gist of this was that the tower, although of rare beauty, had not been much restored since the Saxons built it and the Normans added the finishing touches. Fifty thousand pounds was needed for essential repairs, and the thermometer, erected for the appeal outside the church, was stuck at a low hundred and twenty, the result of an emergency jumble sale.

'You particularly wanted Horace to come this Christmas?' Hilda asked the Man of God with the air of someone anxious to solve a baffling mystery. 'I wonder why that was.'

'Yes. I wonder!' Eric looked startled. 'I wonder why on earth I wanted to ask Horace. I don't believe he's got fifty thousand smackers in his back pocket!' At this, he shook with laughter.

'There,' I told him, 'your lack of faith is entirely justified.' I wasn't exactly enjoying Coldsands Rectory, but I was a little miffed that the Reverend couldn't remember why he'd asked me there in the first place.

'We had hoped that Donald Compton would help us out,' Poppy told us. 'I mean, he wouldn't notice fifty thousand. But he took exception to what Eric said at the Remembrance Day service.'

'Armistice Day in the village,' Eric's grey wings of hair trembled as he nodded in delighted affirmation, 'and I prayed for dead German soldiers. It seemed only fair.'

'Fair perhaps, darling. But hardly tactful,' his wife told him. 'Donald Compton thought it was distinctly unpatriotic. He's bought the Old Manor House,' she explained to Hilda. From then on the conversation turned exclusively to this Compton and was carried on in the tones of awe and muted wonder in which people always talk about the very rich. Compton, it seemed, after a difficult start in England, had gone to Canada where, during a ten-year stay, he laid the foundations of his fortune. His much younger wife was quite charming, probably Canadian, and not in the least stand-offish. He had built the village hall, the cricket pavilion and a tennis court for the school. Only Eric's unfortunate sympathy for the German dead had caused his bounty to stop short at the church tower.

'I've done hours of hard knee work,' the Rector told us, 'begging the Lord to soften Mr Compton's heart towards our tower. No result so far, I fear.'

Apart from this one lapse, the charming Donald Compton seemed to be the perfect English squire and country gent. I would see him in church on Christmas morning, and we had also been invited for drinks before lunch at the Manor. The Reverend Eric and the smiling Poppy made it sound as though the Pope and the Archbishop of Canterbury would be out with the carol singers and we'd been invited to drop in for high tea at Windsor Castle. I also prayed for a yule log blazing at the Manor so that I could, in the true spirit of Christmas, thaw out gradually.

'Now, as a sign of Christmas fellowship, will you all stand and shake hands with those in front and behind you?' Eric, in full canonicals, standing on the steps in front of the altar, made the suggestion as though he had just thought of the idea. I stood reluctantly. I had found myself a place in church near to a huge, friendly, gently humming, occasionally belching radiator and I was clinging to it and stroking it as though it were a new-found mistress (not that I have much experience of new-, or even old-found mistresses). The man who turned to me from the front row seemed to be equally reluctant. He was, as Hilda had pointed out excitedly, the great Donald Compton in person: a man of middle height with silver hair, dressed in a tweed suit and with a tan which it must have been expensive to preserve at Christmas. He had soft brown eyes which looked, almost at once, away from me as, with a touch of his dry fingers, he was gone and I was left for the rest of the service with no more than a well-tailored back and the sound of an uncertain tenor voice joining in the hymns.

I turned to the row behind to shake hands with an elderly woman who had madness in her eyes and whispered conspiratorially to me, 'You cold, dear? Like to borrow my gloves? We're used to a bit of chill weather round these parts.' I declined politely and went back to hugging the radiator, and as I did so a sort of happiness stole over me. To start with, the church was beautiful, with a high timbered roof and walls of weathered stone, peppered with marble tributes to dead inhabitants of the manor. It was decorated with holly and mistletoe, a tree glowed and there were candles over a crib. I thought how many generations of Coldsands villagers, their eyes bright and faces flushed with the wind, had belted out the hymns. I also thought how depressed the great Donald Compton – who had put on little gold half-glasses to read the prophecy from Isaiah: 'For unto us a child is born, unto us a son is given: and the government shall be upon his shoulder: and his name shall be called "Wonderful" – would feel if Jesus's instruction to sell all and give it to the poor should ever be taken literally.

And then I wondered why it was that, as he touched my fingers and turned away, I felt that I had lived through that precise moment before.

There was, in fact, a huge log fire crackling and throwing a dancing light on the marble floor of the circular entrance hall, with its great staircase leading up into private shadows. The cream of Coldsands was being entertained to champagne and canapés by the new Lord of the Manor. The decibels rose as the champagne went down and the little group began to sound like an army of tourists in the Sistine Chapel, noisy, excited and wonderstruck.

'They must be all his ancestors.' Hilda was looking at the pictures and, in particular, at a general in a scarlet coat on a horse prancing in front of some distant battle.

My mouth was full of cream cheese enveloped in smoked salmon. I swallowed it and said, 'Oh, I shouldn't think so. After all, he only bought the house recently.'

'But I expect he brought his family portraits here from somewhere else.'

'You mean, he had them under the bed in his old bachelor

flat in Wimbledon and now he's hung them round an acre or
two of walls?'

'Do try and be serious, Rumpole, you're not nearly as funny
as you think you are. Just look at the family resemblance. I'm
absolutely certain that all of these are old Comptons.'

And it was when she said that that I remembered everything
perfectly clearly.

He was with his wife. She was wearing a black velvet dress
and had long, golden hair that sparkled in the firelight. They
were talking to a bald, pink-faced man and his short and
dumpy wife, and they were all laughing. Compton's laughter
stopped as he saw me coming towards him. He said, 'I don't
think we've met.'

'Yes,' I replied. 'We shook hands briefly in church this
morning. My name's Rumpole and I'm staying with the Long-
staffs. But didn't we meet somewhere else?'

'Good old Eric! We have our differences, of course, but
he's a saintly man. This is my wife Lorelei, and Colonel and
Maudy Jacobs. I expect you'd like to see the library, wouldn't
you, Rumpole? I'm sure you're interested in ancient history.
Will you all excuse us?'

It was two words from Hilda that had done it: 'old' and
'Compton'. I knew then what I should have remembered
when we touched hands in the pews, that Old Compton is a
street in Soho, and that was perhaps why Riccardo (known
as Dicko) Perducci had adopted the name. And I had received
that very same handshake, a slight touch and a quick turn
away when I said goodbye to him in the cells under the Old
Bailey and left him to start seven years for blackmail. The
trial had ended, I now remembered, just before a long-distant
Christmas.

The Perducci territory had been, in those days, not rolling Norfolk acres but a number of Soho strip clubs and clip joints. Girls would stand in front of these last-named resorts and beckon the lonely, the desperate and the unwary in. Sometimes they would escape after paying twenty pounds for a watery cocktail. Unlucky, affluent and important customers might even get sex, carefully recorded by microphones and cameras to produce material which was used for systematic and highly profitable blackmail. The victim in Dicko's case was an obscure and not much loved Circus Judge; so it was regarded as particularly serious by the prosecuting authority.

When I mitigated for Dicko, I stressed the lack of direct evidence against him. He was a shadowy figure who kept himself well in the background and was known as a legend rather than a familiar face round Soho. 'That only shows what a big wheel he was,' Judge Bullingham, who was unfortunately trying the case, bellowed unsympathetically. In desperation I tried the approach of Christmas on him. 'Crimes forgiven, sins remitted, mercy triumphant, such was the message of the story that began in Bethlehem,' I told the Court, at which the Mad Bull snorted that, as far as he could remember, that story ended in a criminal trial and a stiff sentence on at least one thief.

'I suppose something like this was going to happen sooner or later.' We were standing in the library, in front of a comforting fire and among leather-bound books, which I strongly suspected had been bought by the yard. The new, like the old, Dicko was soft-eyed, quietly spoken, almost unnaturally calm; the perfect man behind the scenes of a blackmailing operation or a country estate.

'Not necessarily,' I told him. 'It's just that my wife has so many old school friends and Poppy Longstaff is one of them. Well now, you seem to have done pretty well for yourself. Solid citizens still misconducting themselves round Old Compton Street, are they?'

'I wouldn't know. I gave all that up and went into the property business.'

'Really? Where did you do that? Canada?'

'I never saw Canada.' He shook his head. 'Garwick Prison. Up-and-coming area in the Home Counties. The screws there were ready and willing to do the deals on the outside. I paid them embarrassingly small commissions.'

'How long were you there?'

'Four years. By the time I came out I'd got my first million.'

'Well, then I did you a good turn, losing your case. A bit of luck His Honour Judge Bullingham didn't believe in the remission of sins.'

'You think I got what I deserved?'

I stretched my hands to the fire. I could hear the cocktail chatter from the marble hall of the eighteenth-century manor. 'Treat every man according to his deserts and who shall escape whipping?' I quoted *Hamlet* at him.

'Then I can trust you, Rumpole? The Lord Chancellor's going to put me on the local Bench.'

'The Lord Chancellor lives in a world of his own.'

'You don't think I'd do well as a magistrate?'

'I suppose you'd speak from personal experience of crime. And have some respect for the quality of mercy.'

'I've got no time for that, Rumpole.' His voice became quieter but harder, the brown eyes lost their softness: that, I thought, was how he must have looked when one of his clip-joint girls was caught with the punters' cash stuffed in her tights. 'It's about time we cracked down on crime. Well now, can I trust you not to go out there and spread the word about the last time we met?'

'That depends.'

'On what?'

'How well you have understood the Christmas message.'

'Which is?'

'Perhaps, generosity.'

'I see. So you want your bung?'

'Oh, not me, Dicko. I've been paid, inadequately, by Legal Aid. But there's an impoverished church tower in urgent need of resuscitation.'

'That Eric Longstaff, our Rector – he's not a patriot!'

'And are you?'

'I do a good deal of work locally for the British Legion.'

'And I'm sure, next Poppy Day, they'll appreciate what you've done for the church tower.'

He looked at me for a long minute in silence, and I thought that if this scene had been taking place in a back room in Soho there might, quite soon, have been the flash of a knife. Instead, his hand went to an inside pocket, but it produced nothing more lethal than a cheque book.

'While you're in a giving mood,' I said, 'the Rectory's in desperate need of central heating.'

'This is bloody blackmail!' Dicko Perducci, now known as Donald Compton, said.

'Well,' I told him, 'you should know.'

Christmas was over. The year turned, stirred itself and opened its eyes on a bleak January. Crimes were committed, arrests were made and the courtrooms were filled, once again, with the sound of argument. I went down to the Old Bailey on a trifling matter of fixing the date of a trial before Mrs Justice

Erskine-Brown. As I was leaving, the usher came and told me that the Judge wanted to see me in her private room on a matter of urgency.

Such summonses always fill me with apprehension and a vague feeling of guilt. What had I done? Got the date of the trial hopelessly muddled? Addressed the Court with my trousers carelessly unzipped? I was relieved when the learned Phillida greeted me warmly and even offered me a glass of sherry, poured from her own personal decanter. 'It was so kind of you to offer, Rumpole,' she said unexpectedly.

'Offer what?' I was puzzled.

'You told us how much you adored the traditional British pantomime.'

'So I did.' For a happy moment I imagined Her Ladyship as Principal Boy, her shapely legs encased in black tights, her neat little wig slightly askew, slapping her thigh and calling out, in bell-like tones, 'Cheer up, Rumpole, Portia's not far away.'

'The twins are looking forward to it enormously.'

'Looking forward to what?'

'*Aladdin* at the Tufnell Park Empire. I've got the tickets for the nineteenth of Jan. You do remember promising to take them, don't you?'

'Well, of course.' What else might I have said after the fifth glass of the Erskine-Brown St Emillion? 'I'd love to be of the party. And will old Claude be buying us a dinner afterwards?'

'I really don't think you should go round calling people "old", Rumpole.' Phillida now looked miffed, and I downed the sherry before she took it into her head to deprive me of it. 'Claude's got us tickets for Pavarotti. *L'Elisir d'Amore.* You might buy the children a burger after the show. Oh, and it's not far from us on the Tube. It really was sweet of you to invite them.'

At which she smiled at me and refilled my glass in a way which made it clear she was not prepared to hear further argument.

It all turned out better than I could have hoped. Tristan and Isolde, unlike their Wagnerian namesakes, were cheerful, reasonably polite and seemed only too anxious to dissociate themselves, as far as possible, from the old fart who was escorting them. At every available opportunity they would touch me for cash and then scamper off to buy ice cream, chocolates, sandwiches or Sprite. I was left in reasonable peace to enjoy the performance.

And enjoy it I did. Aladdin was a personable young woman with an upturned nose, a voice which could have been used to wake up patients coming round from their anaesthetics, and memorable thighs. Uncle Abanazer was played, Isolde told me, by an actor known as a social worker with domestic problems in a long-running television series. Wishy and Washy did sing to electric guitars (deafeningly amplified) but Widow Twankey, played by a certain Jim Diamond, was all a Dame should be, a nimble little cockney, fitted up with a sizeable false bosom, a flaming red wig, sweeping eyelashes and scarlet lips. Never have I heard the immortal line, 'Where's that naughty boy Aladdin got to?' better delivered. I joined in loudly (Tristan and Isolde sat silent and embarrassed) when the Widow and Aladdin conducted us in the singing of 'Please Don't Pinch My Tomatoes'. It was, in fact and in fairness, all a traditional pantomime should be, and yet I had a vague feeling that something was wrong, an element was missing. But, as the cast came down a white staircase in glittering costumes to enthusiastic applause, it seemed the sort of pantomime I'd grown up with, and which Tristan and Isolde should be content to inherit.

After so much excitement I felt in need of a stiff brandy and soda, but the eatery the children had selected for their evening's entertainment had apparently gone teetotal and alcohol was not on the menu. Once they were confronted by their mammoth burgers and fries I made my excuses, said I'd be back in a moment, and slipped into the nearby pub which was, I noticed, opposite the stage door of the Empire.

As the life-giving draught was being poured I found myself standing next to Washy and Uncle Abanazer, now out of costume, who were discussing Jim the Dame. 'Very unfriendly tonight,' Washy said. 'Locked himself in his dressing-room before the show and won't join us for a drink.'

'Perhaps he's had a bust-up with Molly?'

'Unlikely. Molly and Jim never had a cross word.'

'Lucky she's never found out he's been polishing Aladdin's wonderful lamp,' Abanazer said, and they both laughed.

And as I asked the girl behind the bar to refill my glass, in which the tide had sunk to a dangerous low, I heard them laugh again about the Widow Twankey's voluminous bosom. 'Strapped-on polystyrene,' Abanazer was saying. 'Almost bruises me when I dance with her. Funny thing, tonight it was quite soft.'

'Perhaps she borrowed one from a blow-up woman?' Washy was laughing as I gulped my brandy and legged it back to the hamburgers. In the dark passage outside the stage door I saw a small, nimble figure in hurried retreat: Jim Diamond, who for some reason hadn't wanted to join the boys at the bar.

After I had restored the children to the Erskine-Browns' au

pair, I sat in the Tube on my way back to Gloucester Road and read the programme. Jim Diamond, it seemed, had started his life in industry before taking up show business. He had a busy career in clubs and turned down appearances on television. ' "I only enjoy the living show," Jim says. "I want to have the audience where I can see them." ' His photograph, without the exaggerated female make-up, showed a pale, thin-nosed, in some way disagreeable little man with a lip curled either in scorn or triumph. I wondered how such an unfriendly-looking character could become an ebullient and warm-hearted widow. Stripped of his make-up, there was something about this comic's unsmiling face which brought back memories of another meeting in totally different circumstances. It was the second time within a few weeks that I had found an old familiar face cast in a new and unexpected part.

The idea, the memory I couldn't quite grasp, preyed on my mind until I was tucked up in bed. Then, as Hilda's latest historical romance dropped from her weary fingers, when she turned her back on me and switched out the light, I saw the face again quite clearly but in a different setting. Not Diamond, not Sparkler, but Sparksman, a logical progression. Widow Twankey had been played by Harry Sparksman, a man who trained as a professional entertainer, if my memory was correct, not in clubs, but in Her Majesty's prisons. It was, it seemed, an interesting career change, but I thought no more of it at the time and, once satisfied with my identification, I fell asleep.

'The boy couldn't have done it, Mr Rumpole. Not a complicated bloody great job to that extent. His only way of getting at a safe was to dig it out of the wall and remove it bodily. He did that in a Barkingside boutique and what he found in it hardly covered the petrol. Young Denis couldn't have got into the Croydon supermarket peter. No one in our family could.'

Uncle Fred, the experienced and cautious head of the Timson clan, had no regard for the safe-breaking talent of Denis, his nephew and, on the whole, an unskilled recruit in the Timson enterprise. The Croydon supermarket job had been highly complicated and expertly carried out and had yielded, to its perpetrators, thousands of pounds. Peanuts Molloy was arrested as one of the lookouts, after falling and twisting an ankle when chased by a night watchman during the getaway. He said he didn't know any of the skilled operators who had engaged him, except Denis Timson who, he alleged, was in general charge of the operation. Denis alone silenced the burglar alarm and deftly penetrated the lock on the safe with an oxyacetylene blowtorch.

It had to be remembered, though, that the clan Molloy had been sworn enemies of the Timson family from time immemorial. Peanuts' story sounded implausible when I met Denis Timson in the Brixton Prison interview room. A puzzled twenty-five-year-old with a shaven head and a poor attempt at a moustache, he seemed more upset by his Uncle Fred's low opinion of him than the danger of a conviction and subsequent prolonged absence from the family.

Denis's case was to come up for committal at the South London Magistrates' Court before 'Skimpy' Simpson, whose lack of success at the Bar had driven him to a job as a stipendiary beak. His nickname had been earned by the fact that he had not, within living memory, been known to splash out on a round of drinks in Pommeroy's Wine Bar.

In the usual course of events, there is no future in fighting proceedings which are only there to commit the customer to trial. I had resolved to attend solely to pour a little well-deserved contempt on the evidence of Peanuts Molloy. As I started to prepare the case, I made a note of the date of the Croydon supermarket break-in. As soon as I had done so, I consulted my diary. I turned the virgin pages as yet unstained by notes of trials, ideas for cross-examinations, splodges of tea or spilled glasses of Pommeroy's Very Ordinary. It was as I had thought. While some virtuoso was at work on the Croydon safe, I was enjoying *Aladdin* in the company of Tristan and Isolde.

'Detective Inspector Grimble. Would you agree that whoever blew the safe in the Croydon supermarket did an extraordinarily skilful job?'

'Mr Rumpole, are we meant to congratulate your client on his professional skill?'

God moves in a mysterious way, and it wasn't Skimpy Simpson's fault that he was born with thin lips and a voice which sounded like the rusty hinge of a rusty gate swinging in the wind. I decided to ignore him and concentrate on a friendly chat with D. I. Grimble, a large, comfortable, ginger-haired officer. We had lived together, over the years, with the clan Timson and their mis-doings. He was known to them as a decent and fair-minded cop, as disapproving of the younger, Panda-racing, evidence-massaging intake to the Force as they were of the lack of discretion and criminal skills which marked the younger Timsons.

'I mean the thieves were well informed. They knew that there would be a week's money in the safe.'

'They knew that, yes.'

'And was there a complex burglar-alarm system? You couldn't put it out of action simply by cutting wires, could you?'

'Cutting the wires would have set it off.'

'So putting the burglar alarm out of action would have required special skills?'

'It would have done.'

'Putting it out of action also stopped a clock in the office. So we know that occurred at eight-forty-five?'

'We know that. Yes.'

'And at nine-twenty young Molloy was caught as he fell, running to a getaway car.'

'That is so.'

'So this heavy safe was burnt open in a little over half an hour?'

'I fail to see the relevance of that, Mr Rumpole.' Skimpy was getting restless.

'I'm sure the officer does. That shows a very high degree of technical skill, doesn't it, Detective Inspector?'

'I'd agree with that.'

'Exercised by a highly experienced peterman?'

'Who is this Mr Peterman?' Skimpy was puzzled. 'We haven't heard of him before.'

'Not Mr Peterman.' I marvelled at the ignorance of the basic facts of life displayed by the magistrate. 'A man expert at blowing safes, known to the trade as "peters",' I told him and turned back to D. I. Grimble. 'So we're agreed that this was a highly expert piece of work?'

'It must have been done by someone who knew his job pretty well. Yes.'

'Denis Timson's record shows convictions for shoplifting, bag-snatching and stealing a radio from an unlocked car. In all of these simple enterprises, he managed to get caught.'

'Your client's criminal record!' Skimpy looked happy for the first time. 'You're allowing that to go into evidence, are you, Mr Rumpole?'

'Certainly, Sir.' I explained the obvious point. 'Because there's absolutely no indication he was capable of blowing a safe in record time, or silencing a complicated burglar-alarm, is there, Detective Inspector?'

'No. There's nothing to show anything like that in his record . . .'

'Mr Rumpole,' Skimpy was looking at the clock; was he in danger of missing his usual train back home to Haywards Heath? 'Where's all this heading?'

'Back a good many years,' I told him, 'to the Sweet-Home Building Society job at Carshalton. When Harry Sparksman blew a safe so quietly that even the dogs slept through it.'

'You were in that case, weren't you, Mr Rumpole?' Inspector Grimble was pleased to remember. 'Sparksman got five years.'

'Not one of your great successes.' Skimpy was also delighted. 'Perhaps you wasted the Court's time with unnecessary questions. Have you anything else to ask this officer?'

'Not till the Old Bailey, Sir. I may have thought of a few more by then.'

With great satisfaction, Skimpy committed Denis Timson, a minor villain who would have had difficulty changing a fuse, let alone blowing a safe, for trial at the Central Criminal Court.

'Funny you mentioned Harry Sparksman. Do you know, the same thought occurred to me. An expert like him could've done that job in the time.'

'Great minds think alike,' I assured D. I. Grimble. We were washing away the memory of an hour or two before

Skimpy with two pints of nourishing stout in the pub opposite the beak's Court. 'You know Harry took up a new career?' I needn't have asked the question. D. I. Grimble had a groupie's encyclopaedic knowledge of the criminal stars.

'Oh yes. Now a comic called Jim Diamond. Got up a concert party in the nick. Apparently gave him a taste for show business.'

'I did hear,' I took Grimble into my confidence, 'that he made a come-back for the Croydon job.' It had been a throwaway line from Uncle Fred Timson – 'I heard talk they got Harry back out of retirement' – but it was a thought worth examining.

'I heard the same. So we did a bit of checking. But Sparksman, known as Diamond, has got a cast-iron alibi.'

'Are you sure?'

'The time when the Croydon job was done, he was performing in a pantomime. On stage nearly all the evening, it seems, playing the Dame.'

'*Aladdin*,' I said, 'at the Tufnell Park Empire. It might just be worth your while to go into that alibi a little more thoroughly. I'd suggest you have a private word with Mrs Molly Diamond. It's just possible she may have noticed his attraction to Aladdin's lamp.'

'Now then, Mr Rumpole,' Grimble was wiping the froth from his lips with a neatly folded handkerchief, 'you mustn't tell me how to do my job.'

'I'm only trying to serve,' I managed to look pained, 'the interests of justice!'

'You mean, the interests of your client?'

'Sometimes they're the same thing,' I told him, but I had to admit it wasn't often.

As it happened, the truth emerged without Detective Inspector Grimble having to do much of a job. Harry had, in fact, fallen victim to a tip-tilted nose and memorable thighs; he'd left home and moved into Aladdin's Kensal Rise flat. Molly, taking a terrible revenge, blew his alibi wide open. She had watched many rehearsals and knew every word, every gag, every nudge, wink and shrill complaint of the Dame's part. She had played it to perfection to give her husband an alibi while he went back to his old job in Croydon. It all went perfectly, even though Uncle Abanazer, dancing with her, had felt an unexpected softness.

I had known, instinctively, that something was very wrong. It had, however, taken some time for me to realize what I had really seen that night at the Tufnell Park Empire. It was nothing less than an outrage to a Great British Tradition. The Widow Twankey was a woman.

D. I. Grimble made his arrest and the case against Denis Timson was dropped by the Crown Prosecution Service. As spring came to the Temple gardens, Hilda opened a letter in the other case which turned on the recognition of old, familiar faces and read it out to me.

'The repointing's going well on the tower and we hope to have it finished by Easter,' Poppy Longstaff had written. 'And I have to tell you, Hilda, the oil-fired heating has changed our lives. Eric says it's like living in the tropics. Cooking supper last night, I had to peel off at least one of my cardigans.' She Who Must Be Obeyed put down the letter from her old school friend and said, thoughtfully, 'Noblesse Oblige.'

'What was that, Hilda?'

'I could tell at once that Donald Compton was a true gentleman. The sort that does good by stealth. Of course, poor old Eric thought he'd never get the tower mended, but I somehow felt that Donald wouldn't fail him. It was noblesse.'

'Perhaps it was,' I conceded, 'but in this case the noblesse was Rumpole's.'

'Rumpole! What on earth do you mean? You hardly paid to have the church tower repointed, did you?'

'In one sense, yes.'

'I can't believe that. After all the years it took you to have the bathroom decorated. What on earth do you mean about *your* noblesse?'

'It'd take too long to explain, old darling. Besides, I've got a conference in Chambers. Tricky case of receiving stolen surgical appliances. I suppose,' I added doubtfully, 'it may lead, at some time in the distant future, to an act of charity.'

Easter came, the work on the tower was successfully completed, and I was walking back to Chambers after a gruelling day down the Bailey when I saw, wafting through the Temple cloisters, the unlikely apparition of the Rev. Eric Longstaff. He chirruped a greeting and said he'd come up to consult some legal brains on the proper investment of what remained of the Church Restoration Fund. 'I'm so profoundly grateful,' he told me, 'that I decided to invite you down to the Rectory last Christmas.'

'*You* decided?'

'Of course I did.'

'I thought your wife Poppy extended the invitation to She . . .'

'Oh yes. But I thought of the idea. It was the result of a good deal of hard knee-work and guidance from above. I knew you were the right man for the job.'

'What job?'

'The Compton job.'

What was this? The Rector was speaking like an old con. The Coldsands caper? 'What *can* you mean?'

'I just mean that I knew you'd defended Donald Compton. In a previous existence.'

'How on earth did you know that?'

Eric drew himself up to his full, willowy height. 'I'm not a prison visitor for nothing,' he said proudly, 'so I thought you were just the chap to put the fear of God into him. You were the very person to put the squeeze on the Lord of the Manor.'

'Put the squeeze on him?' Words were beginning to fail me.

'That was the idea. It came to me as a result of knee-work.'

'So you brought us down to that freezing Rectory just so I could blackmail the local benefactor?'

'Didn't it turn out well!'

'May the Lord forgive you.'

'He's very forgiving.'

'Next time,' I spoke to the Man of God severely, 'the Church can do its blackmailing for itself.'

'Oh, we're quite used to that.' The Rector smiled at me in what I thought was a lofty manner. 'Particularly around Christmas.'

Rumpole and the Remembrance of Things Past

There are no sadder relics of the past than the rows of small, semi-detached houses that line one of the western approaches to London. Once they were lived in and alive. Minis were washed on Sunday mornings inside their lean-to garages, bright dahlias and tea roses grew in their front gardens, their doorbells chimed and, on winter evenings, lights glowed from the stained-glass portholes in their front doors.

Now their blind windows are stuffed with hardboard, their front doors nailed up, their gardens piled with rubble and their garages collapsed. They are derelict victims of a long-delayed scheme to widen the main road, and some of these houses have already been pulled out like rotten teeth. When it came to be the turn of 35 Primrose Drive, a digger, prising up the sitting-room floor, lifted, with apparent tenderness, the well-preserved and complete skeleton of a young woman. Reports were made to the police and the coroner's office. D. I. Winthrop, an enthusiastic young officer, started an inquiry which led, to his great satisfaction, to the arrest of William Twineham, the sole owner of the house since its birth in the sixties. Twineham's wife Josephine had, the D. I. discovered, vanished unaccountably some thirty-three years previously.

★

I was standing outside my Chambers in Equity Court, wearing my hat to protect the thinning top of my head from the drizzle and thinking, as my old darling Wordsworth would say, of old, unhappy, far-off things and crimes so long ago.

Around me in the doorways, under the arches or leaning against a sheltered wall, were many poor souls like me, driven out of doors. Most of them were girls. Short-skirted, high-heeled, with cigarettes dangling from their lips, they would seem to any passer-by to be ladies of the street, and the same casual observer might have been forgiven for supposing that the Outer Temple, home of the legal profession, had become a red-light district in the manner of downtown Amsterdam. The casual observer would have been wrong. Neither they nor I were out of doors to offer sexual services. We were temporary exiles from Chambers which had become smoke-free zones.

The Inn was all for it, as was Soapy Sam Ballard. Mizz Liz Probert, who has now taken to coming to work on a daunting motorbike which pumps more gas into the atmosphere than a lifetime's small cigars, went over to the Green Party. Claude Erskine-Brown blamed my cheroots for the fact that his aunt had been flooded out by a climate change in Surrey. In vain I argued for the democratic rights of minorities. The smoking ban was introduced by a tyrannical majority, so I basked in the warmth of a small cigar as the rain settled in the brim of my hat.

'Loitering with intent, Rumpole?'

'Still polluting the atmosphere . . . ?'

Two grey, almost ghost-like figures approached through the rain. They were the opera-loving, wine-tasting, inadequate advocate Claude Erskine-Brown and none other than Soapy Sam Ballard, the unworthy Head of my Chambers.

These were the two who had undertaken to save the planet earth from extinction by kicking Rumpole, and our junior secretary Dawn, out into a storm to have a puff, an act which, in my humble submission, bore a close resemblance to the way Goneril and Regan treated their old Dad.

'I'm glad you're showing some respect for the rules, Rumpole. Respect for the rules is the vital ingredient of a happy ship.'

'What do you mean, respect for the rules?' I found Ballard's description of me as a rules respecter particularly offensive. 'I simply came out here to think.'

'Oh, really?' Erskine-Brown was unconvinced. 'What were you thinking about, exactly?'

'Skeletons. And how many family homes in respectable areas may have skeletons under the floorboards. God knows what goes on behind the double locks and burglar alarms. Have you ever looked under your floorboards, Ballard?'

The question, I was glad to see, had Soapy Sam looking momentarily worried. Erskine-Brown, like a faithful hound, came to his master's rescue with a piece of irrelevant information. 'You just put one of those disgusting whiffs into your mouth, Rumpole. You clearly came out here to smoke.'

'I came out here to be alone,' I assured the man with what dignity I could muster. 'Clearly I failed miserably.'

'Just try and remember – smoke causes global warming *even out of doors*. Did you see the pictures of Godalming?'

'No, I didn't. I don't go about searching for pictures of Godalming, Erskine-Brown.'

'My aunt,' Claude's voice sank to the doom-laden level of a news reader announcing the end of the world, 'had to be taken shopping in a collapsible canoe.'

★

'Here's your man, Mr Rumpole.'

The screw on duty at the Brixton interview room was used to delivering a succession of alleged murderers, rapists and receivers of stolen laptops to me and my faithful instructing solicitor, 'Bonny' Bernard, where a chair awaited them by the Formica-covered table which bore my brief, Bernard's packet of courtesy Marlboro Lights and the top of a tin of Oxo cubes which served as an ashtray.

The captive now delivered was markedly different from the usual run of Rumpole's clientele, in that he was neither angry, cocky, chippy nor overly anxious to please his brief. He didn't, as some customers do, appear eager to pretend that his dire situation was a bit of a joke. To begin with he was tall, well over six foot, causing me to look up at him. He was old, I should have said in his late sixties. He was also handsome, with clear-cut features, unblinking blue eyes and a head of white hair, well brushed, as perhaps his only vanity. He stood looking at me and Bonny Bernard with the half-smile of an Old Testament prophet who had arrived in Gomorrah and found it just as sad and disgusting as he had been led to believe.

'Sit down, Mr Twineham.' I waved him to a chair. 'Do have one of Mr Bernard's cigarettes.'

'Thank you. I do not care to pollute the lovely world the good Lord has given us.' Another of them! I accepted the fact, then I thought that at least no one in prison had to go out into the street to smoke.

'This is Mr Rumpole.' Mr Bernard made the introduction. 'He'll be defending you at the trial.'

'The Lord has sent you.' William Twineham looked at me as though he had been given a warning of my arrival into his life and thought there was, after all, nothing much he could do about it. 'It's not for me to question the inscrutable ways of Providence.'

'You and your wife moved into number 35 Primrose Drive, as I understand, as soon as it was built.' It was time, I thought, to move away from the concerns of God to such mundane details as might interest an Old Bailey Jury.

'Certainly. She was known as Jo in certain quarters.' And then the alleged murderer gave us a sudden smile. It was modest, unexpectedly charming and seemed to illuminate the shadowy interview room. 'To me she was always Josephine.' He said it tenderly; whether he meant it or was treating us to an expert professional performance was not yet clear.

'So there were no previous occupants of the house?' No one else, was what I meant, to have stowed an unwanted wife under the floorboards.

'We watched it being built after we'd put down our deposit. It was to be our house together for the next five years.'

'And your home until the Council took over all the houses. You lived there alone?'

'I still felt Josephine was there. The memories.'

'In fact she left you in 1968. I'm looking at the statement of Paul and Louisa Arkwright, your semi-detached neighbours. You told them you didn't know where your wife had gone. Or with whom?'

'I told them that. Yes!'

'Was that true?'

'It seemed true. She had left me!'

'What does that mean – "seemed"?'

'How much can we ever truly know, Mr Rumpole, this side of the grave? When we see through a glass darkly.'

Looking at the next-door neighbours' statements, I felt I could see through a glass altogether too clearly.

'The Arkwrights say they heard sounds of a violent quarrel shortly before your wife disappeared. Is that true . . . ?'

William Twineham's smile died. His eyes were closed, his body moved as though in time to unheard music as he recited in a muted singsong, 'And to the woman were given two wings of a great eagle, that she might fly into the wilderness, into her place, where she is nourished for a time, and times, and half a time from the face of the serpent.'

'Who said that?'

'Saint John the Divine.'

'What's it meant to mean?'

'We must wait, Mr Rumpole, you and I must wait, until all things are made clear.'

'We can't wait, I'm afraid.' Bonny Bernard seemed to have found the Book of Revelations singularly unrevealing. 'Your trial's fixed for Tuesday the seventeenth. We've got just about three weeks.'

But I was looking back over thirty-three years. I had the prosecution album of photographs. The first was taken from one framed on William Twineham's mantelpiece in the bedsit he had moved to when number 35 was taken over. I saw a girl laughing, with long, curly hair, which shone on some faraway summer afternoon, crowned with a daisy chain. I turned the page, and there on a mortuary table was the completely reassembled skeleton, the empty ribcage, the skull with dark sockets, all that was left of Josephine Twineham, known to everyone except her husband as Jo.

I took a deep breath and tried again. 'Mr Twineham, I don't know exactly what your religious beliefs might be . . .'

'He regularly attends his church in Pinner.' Bernard had a note in his file.

'The True Church Apostolic. I know nothing of *your* religious beliefs, Mr Rumpole.'

I wondered how much I knew myself. My creed included a simple faith in trial by Jury and the presumption of innocence. The eleventh commandment was, 'Thou Shalt Not Plead Guilty'. I had a faint hope that the Day of Judgment, if there was ever to be a Day of Judgment, would not entail a day in Court as ferocious and unjust as a bad time before Judge Bullingham down the Old Bailey. I decided to avoid the issue. 'I don't think my beliefs are strictly relevant.'

'Beliefs, Mr Rumpole,' our client was smiling again now, 'are always relevant. My church has taught me to interpret Revelations and understand the gift of prophecy.'

'Then perhaps you will reveal this to us. Did you kill your wife?'

Mr Twineham was looking at me steadily, his smile undimmed. 'Josephine's death was an act of God.'

'And did you give God any sort of assistance at the time?'

Instead of a smile, I got another question. 'Does anyone say I did?'

'You quarrelled. She disappeared. She seems to have been found buried under the hearth in your living-room. They will ask the Jury to draw the inference that you killed her.'

'You mean, ask them to guess?'

'An informed guess. Yes. That's what they'll decide. Unless you tell them a different story.'

'What sort of story would you suggest?'

This was blasphemy! My religious beliefs, such as they are, had been deeply insulted. As an old black cab plying for hire, I had been engaged by some pretty dubious customers, shysters, fraudsters and con men to whom the truth was, like the Virgin Birth, a remote myth. But I had never met a customer who had asked me to invent a defence for him, nor would I ever have consented to do so. Fired by indignation, I asked an unusual and risky question. 'How about telling me the truth?'

'About the night Josephine and I quarrelled?'

'All about it.'

'What happened that night . . . is one of the mysteries.'

'Juries don't like mysteries.'

'How much should I tell? I shall pray for guidance.'

'Well, all I can say is do it soon. Otherwise I'll give you a prophecy to think about.'

'What is your prophecy?' For the first time, our client seemed genuinely interested in what I had to say.

'I see,' I told William Twineham, 'through a glass and not so darkly, you spending most of your remaining life locked in a cell, probably with some unstable psychopathic killer, in a sink prison with drug dealing, unchecked violence and screws who may take an instant dislike to you. So get your guidance, return of post, and we'll be back.'

'Oh yes,' Bernard told him forcefully, gathering up his papers, 'we'll be back.'

'Have you finished, Mr Rumpole?' A screw opened the glass door and enquired politely.

'Not really. In fact we've hardly begun.' And so we left William Twineham to his prayers.

'Thirty-three years ago. Just imagine what it'd be like to be tried for something after all those years, perhaps when you were an entirely different person.' What had that overworked, meticulous and respectable solicitor Mr Bernard done some forty years ago that he wouldn't have liked to admit to in Court? It wasn't long after the disappearance of Jo that we first met. What was the first case he sent me? One of the Timson clan, now grey-haired and walking with the aid of a stick, sowing his wild oats in the theft of lead off a church roof.

'I mean, Will Twineham must have thought the past was all over,' Bernard went on. 'Dead and buried.'

'To coin a phrase,' I muttered, refilling our glasses from the bottle of Château Thames Embankment which Jack Pommeroy had agreed to put on my somewhat overcrowded slate. 'You're right, though. If some remote town-planner or some faceless committee hadn't decided to widen the road into London, Jo Twineham would have slept under the floor undisturbed and our client could remain a pillar of the Apostolic Church.'

'It's the shock of that all coming out that's turned his mind, wouldn't you reckon?'

'Either that or he's decided to take cover behind the Book of Revelations.'

'The evidence of identification,' Bernard tried to sound helpful, 'it's not all that convincing.'

'You mean some complete stranger might have broken into the house and buried a woman we know absolutely nothing about in the front parlour? I know you're trying to be helpful . . .'

'That line's no use to us?'

'Probably not. What I'd like most is . . .'

'Is what, Mr Rumpole?'

'To get to know him. To get to know both of them, in fact. He's so serious and she was so beautiful. What did they quarrel about àll those years ago?'

Before Mr Bernard could offer any help, we were rudely interrupted by a voice crying from the other end of the bar, in a penetrating Welsh accent, 'It's Roly Poly Rumpole, by all that's wonderful!'

I looked round to find myself being approached by a stranger with a toothy grin, strong bifocals and a shock of blond hair going grey. He had, in spite of his age, the cheerful look of a schoolboy in some long-gone comic, famous for his jolly japes and teasing of housemasters.

'Owen Oswald! Remember me, don't you?'

'I'm afraid I don't.'

'Dangerous driving. Swansea. 1981. You defended me. I chose you.'

He had advanced and was very close to me, one hand gripping my lapel as though to hold himself upright and breathing out the sweet smell of gin and tonic. 'I chose you because my solicitor said you'd get the whole bench of magistrates laughing my case out. Said you were a dab hand with the jokes, if you know what I mean.'

'I know exactly what you mean. So did I get them laughing?'

'You did, my dear old Roly Poly. You most certainly did. And when you suggested to the other driver that he had his car painted in his *racing* colours . . .'

'They laughed at that?' It sounded improbable.

'Tickled pink, they were.'

'So we won?'

'We didn't win. They enjoyed a good laugh and banned me for two years. Thousand-pound fine. You were the most expensive entertainment I ever went to.'

By now I was anxious to be rid of the Welsh joker with his memories of past failure and get on with Mr Bernard, the bottle of Château Thames Embankment and the fatal relationship of Jo and Will Twineham. But what Owen

Oswald said next grabbed my attention and eventually, I thought, put me permanently in his debt.

'Just up here for a conference on a business matter, and they told me you were in old Bonzo Ballard's Chambers.'

'I am in Chambers supposedly led by a person called Ballard. But I know nothing of "Bonzo".'

'No one calls him Bonzo any more?'

'"Soapy Sam", is that who you mean?'

'It's obvious you weren't at the University of Wales in Cardiff, 1966–69.'

'I have a vague memory of Soapy Sam telling me that the Law Faculty in Cardiff was miles ahead of anything Oxford or Edinburgh had to offer, which is why he'd honoured it with his presence . . .'

'I can't remember him talking much about the law. It was the band. That was the great thing with Bonzo.'

'The band?' What was the fellow talking about – some earnest group dedicated to Christian fellowship? 'What sort of band?'

'Bonzo Ballard and the Pithead Stompers. Enthusiastic but, in my humble opinion, they couldn't hold a candle to The Swinging Blue Jeans, let alone Frank Zappa.'

'Are you telling me that Soapy Sam Ballard played in a band?' I felt, at this moment, some blessed hope of which I had long been unaware.

'All over the place. Uni dances, working men's clubs, Saturday night pubs, old people's homes, till the old people went on strike.'

'Are you telling me that Soapy Sam played some instrument?'

'Slapped away at a guitar. You know the sort of thing. And sang – not badly.'

'Sang?' I couldn't believe my luck. 'Are there no recordings available? Perhaps an old '78?'

'I don't think they were ever let into a recording studio. But I've got a photograph.'

'A photograph – featuring Ballard?'

'A photograph starring Bonzo. He had hair down to his shoulders at the time.'

'You keep it as some sort of memento?'

'I keep it because I was a member of the Pithead Stompers. On drums.'

I looked at the man as a mountaineer clinging to the edge of a cliff might greet the guide come to haul him to safety. 'I'm not a rich man,' I confessed to Oswald. 'I do Legal Aid crime and we only get paid now and then. But I'm prepared to spend good money on a copy of this photograph.'

'I'll send you one.' The rescuing Welshman had his arm round my shoulder. 'You can buy me a drink next time we meet.'

'I think I'm on a winner,' I told Bernard, after I'd given my saviour the Chambers address.

'You mean with Twineham?' He was incredulous.

'No. I mean with Ballard.' But I had earned my solicitor's look of disapproval. I had forgotten a young woman with flowers in her hair, dead and buried under a living-room floor. And all because I was engaged in a fight, with no holds barred, to stop having to smoke small cigars in the rain.

'You've taken on his case, Rumpole?' My wife, Hilda, known to me only as She Who Must Be Obeyed, cross-examined me over the breakfast table.

'He's taken on me.'

'How could you? A man like that!'

'I'm not sure I can manage it,' I confessed to Hilda. 'Apart from quoting the Book of Revelations, he hasn't given me the slightest hint of a defence.'

'I always knew you'd stoop to anything, Rumpole . . . but I never dreamed you'd side with men who bury their wives under the floor!'

What did she think? That I approved in any way of such conduct? That I could ever, in a million years, become such a husband? For a nightmare moment, I pictured myself trying to inter Hilda somehow below the well-worn Axminster, and rejected the idea as a physical impossibility. Then I heard a heavy sigh on the other side of the toast and marmalade. Hilda's mood had swung from the usual brisk attack on Rumpole's conduct to a note of sadness and regret as she looked down at the letter in her hand.

'I can't possibly go now. It would be too embarrassing.'

'You can't go where, Hilda?'

'The Old Saint Elfreda's dinner.'

'But you always go.' It was a reunion Hilda never missed, a party at which her innumerable old schoolfriends relived their gymslip years and which I welcomed as an opportunity for a quietly convivial evening in Pommeroy's Wine Bar.

'Not now. Look at this.' She handed me the embossed invitation as though it were the announcement of a death. 'President of the OEs this year, Lady Shiplake, Chrissie Snelling as was. It's so not fair! She never came to OE reunions, but as she married this Labour Lord, they've made her President. Neither Dodo Mackintosh nor I will be able to go now!'

'Why ever not?'

There was a long and solemn pause, and then Hilda uttered a word which I didn't know existed in her vocabulary.

'Guilt.'

'You mean this Chrissie has a criminal record?'

'No. Dodo and I.'

'Hilda.' The breath had been knocked out of me. 'You're confessing to something?'

'Dodo and I did it together.'

'You were fellow conspirators?'

'We called her Smelling, of course. "Here comes Chrissie Smelling." And we held our noses. We pretended there was a rule that everyone had to run round the hockey field three times before breakfast, and Chrissie did it. We sent her fake Valentine cards, making dates with non-existent chaps from the boys' school. We pinched her knicker linings and punctured her hot-water bottle. Halfway through one term a car with a chauffeur came and took Chrissie away. It was all our fault, Rumpole.'

'Any other offences to be taken into consideration?' I hope I looked suitably shocked.

'I can't think of any more at the moment.'

'It's a formidable charge sheet.'

'I know. Dodo and I simply couldn't face her again. Neither of us could.'

'That's exactly why you've got to go!' For once in my married life, I was occupying the moral high ground, where the air was fresh and intoxicating.

'Oh, Rumpole!' Could it be that She Who Must Be Obeyed was capable of a cry for help? 'Don't make me!'

Could I make her? Could I turn Judge Bullingham into a soft-hearted, do-gooding member of the Howard League for Penal Reform? Of course I couldn't. All the same, I meant to put up a fight for an evening with a few well-chosen solicitors and convivial crime reporters in Pommeroy's.

'I just think,' I gave Hilda the Rumpole look of gentle but

serious concern, 'you have the honour of Saint Elfreda's to consider.'

'Dodo and I have always been intensely loyal to the old school.'

'Always in the past, perhaps. But not now. Or is it part of the Saint Elfreda's tradition to run away from your responsibilities?'

'What do you want me to do, Rumpole?' Another record broken: such a question had never been asked before, in the long, windy history of our married life.

'Face up to it, Hilda. Confess everything and throw yourselves on the mercy of the Court. I am convinced,' and now Rumpole was at his most judicial, 'that you and Dodo Mackintosh will feel the better, the purer for it.'

For a long moment, the fate of my free evening hung in the balance. Then she said, 'I'll ring Dodo and ask her what she thinks.'

'You won't. You'll tell her what you think,' I said, but not out loud. By now, I was satisfied that ringing Dodo would end in a summons to face the music.

'After he had told us that his wife had left home, Will Twineham lived alone. We never saw a sign of another woman or girlfriend staying the night. I must say, he kept the house spotless. There was always a big jug of flowers kept on the hearth of the fireplace in the front room. He bought flowers at the Tube station on his way home from work. Will never lit a fire. It seemed that he could endure any amount of cold. Indeed, he said he enjoyed it.'

I was reading, once again, the statements of the semi-detached neighbours. I thought about flowers in the hearth and couldn't help remembering the flower-sellers at the gates of the great London cemeteries, the dying chrysanthemums and fading daffodils on the granite chips, within the marble frame on the grave. Whilst I was having these disturbing thoughts, the door swung open and Soapy Sam Ballard glided in. 'Rumpole,' he said, 'a word with you.'

'You've come to free us from political correctness? Small cheroots may be lit again in 1 Equity Court?' I asked with quiet confidence.

'Will nothing make you, Rumpole, take some responsibility for the universe?'

'I seem to remember floods in Noah's day, when very few people were smoking whiffs. Have you forgotten your Bible, old darling?'

'Rumpole, please don't quote the Scriptures to excuse your filthy habit.'

'I wouldn't dream of it. I'll only remind you that the commandment "Thou Shalt Not Light Up" appears nowhere, from Genesis to Revelations.'

'If you can be serious for a moment . . .'

'I'll try. If you promise not to make me laugh.'

'This is entirely serious. I heard in the clerks' room that you are defending Twineham.'

'You heard right.'

'A difficult case.'

'One it would be all too easy to lose.'

'Have you got a defence?'

'Not yet. One may come to me if you'd be good enough to tiptoe away and close the door very quietly after you.' I couldn't have put it more plainly, but the man loitered on, like the last guest at a party who wants a bed for the night.

'Two heads, Rumpole, are considerably better than one.'

'Doesn't that rather depend on whose heads they are?'

'I assume that you're not thinking of doing this case alone and without a leader?' Soapy Sam announced the purpose of his visit. He was a QC, a fact which confirmed my definition of the whole genus as 'Queer Customers'. As such, he would be entitled to play the lead in the defence team, leaving Rumpole, one of the oldest and, if I may say it, most accomplished juniors, to carry a spear, in the way of making notes, calling the odd witness and bringing the learned leader's coffee to him. There was clearly no place for Ballard in the curious drama of 35 Primrose Drive.

'I did the Penge Bungalow Murders without a leader when I was an upwardly mobile white-wig. I don't think that, over the years, I've lost any of my powers.'

'I'll ask our clerk to speak to your solicitor. I'm sure he'll be delighted to brief me as your leader.'

'I very much doubt it. Bernard likes to enjoy his cases down the Old Bailey.'

Soapy Sam had nothing more to say. He stood goggling at me for a moment, and then made, slowly and thoughtfully, for the exit.

'Shut the door,' I said, 'Bonzo.'

He froze. His hand poised over the door handle, he turned to me, satisfactorily anxious. 'What did you say?'

'Nothing very much,' I reassured him. It was not yet time to strike. 'I'm sorry. Silly of me. I must have been calling some old dog. Forgot myself for a moment. I'll see you around.'

Soapy Sam gave me a quick stare and left. I had, I felt sure, unnerved the man and fired a warning shot across his brow.

The weighty matter of Hilda's guilt and the consequent acceptance or refusal of the Old Girls' Reunion Dinner invitation was of too earthshaking importance to be decided by one telephone call, however prolonged. An invitation was given, and accepted, from Dodo Mackintosh for a week's visit to Lamorna Cove, where the issue could be tried at length, no doubt over cups of Ovaltine far into the night, and a definite verdict arrived at.

'Will you be all right, Rumpole?' Hilda asked with unusual solicitude, as though afraid I might disappear by chauffeur-driven car and never return to the so-called mansion flat in Froxbury Mansions.

'Quite all right,' I reassured her. 'Take your time, this is not the sort of decision that can be taken in a hurry. Much, including the honour of the old school, depends upon it.'

So, as well as the possibility of an evening off if the dinner was on, I had a whole week on my own. And this was convenient, because Bernard had met a solicitor named Tony Thrale who had revealed, over lunch at the Law Society, that when he was a young articled clerk working and living round Perivale, he had met, in various clubs and all-night parties, Jo Twineham, whose name was now splashed across the tabloids in preparation for the reporting of a sensational murder trial. He had invited us both to dinner, as he thought he might be able to help us, provided we undertook to keep him out of Court.

'Dinner?' I was surprised at this offer of hospitality from a potential witness. 'What's that going to be like?'

'They live in Maida Vale now. It'll be dinner with a big company lawyer. Good food. Handsome wife in a black frock. Candles. After-dinner mints.'

But when we got to the Thrales', it wasn't like that at all.

★

The front door of the sedate Victorian house in Maida Vale opened on to a purple and highly scented darkness. You might have walked from bright sunlight into the shadows of the kasbah. Tony Thrale greeted us. A burly, grey-haired man in his late fifties, he was dressed for dinner in a pair of faded jeans, backless slippers and a shirt which seemed to have once been dyed in various colours that had run into each other.

'Mr Rumpole.' He greeted me, not with the handshake he would no doubt have offered had we met in the course of business, but with a kind of bear-like hug which brought me into close contact with the tie-dyed shirt and some sort of medallion nestling among the grey hairs immediately below his neck. 'I salute you, Mr Rumpole. The only truly free spirit at the Bar. Glenda can't wait to meet you. I told her I was sure you'd be one of us. Vegetarian.'

The heart, I have to confess, sank. Was this what I'd come out for? I remembered, longingly, the remains of a steak and kidney pie waiting for me in the fridge in Froxbury Mansions. Were not free spirits carnivores? I shot an appealing look at Bernard, who was walking, apparently untroubled, towards the pulses.

If Glenda Thrale was anxious to see me, she managed to keep her impatience well under control. Wearing a kaftan, adorned with beads, squatting on what, I believe, during the heyday of such articles was known as a bean bag, she turned on us a look of minimal interest. This was accompanied, certainly, by a faint smile, but then she smiled without interruption during most of our visit. This smile was in no way connected with anything in the smallest degree comic. Indeed, when after what they eccentrically described as 'dinner' was over and I told some of my better courtroom anecdotes, the smile faded on every punch line.

We had been led by Tony Thrale into a kind of cavern, a huge and shadowy open-plan area. At one end of it, illuminated by spotlights, there was a large Aga cooker at which Tony was now boiling up some kind of vegetable matter. The rest of the cave was sporadically illuminated by lamps muffled with heavy shades or, in some cases, swathed in paisley shawls. The smell which had loitered in the hall now intensified and seemed to be compounded of ecclesiastical incense, smouldering carpets and simmering lentils. Music with a loud and insistent beat poured relentlessly out of a 'music centre'.

I had taken my seat next to a purple-fringed shawl and an uncased guitar in the corner of the sofa, while Bernard was balanced, a little unsteadily, on another bean bag. Looking round the room, sniffing the exotic odours, I thought we were in a museum, a careful reproduction of the past, like the Victorian dining-rooms or eighteenth-century boudoirs that might be constructed to educate the public on the way we lived then. Or did Tony Thrale, by all accounts a conventional solicitor by day, come home each evening to life in a time warp?

'Mr Rumpole,' Glenda Thrale was speaking to me in a voice that was curiously high and seemed to come from a long way off, 'don't you adore the Beach Boys?'

Was she casting serious doubt at my sexual orientation? I must say I bridled a little and answered, in an aloof sort of way, 'I'm afraid I don't spend much time on beaches.'

At this Glenda fell into a prolonged silence, and my spirits sank to a new low when Tony offered us, by way of a predinner sharpener, a temperance beverage, a curiously unattractive mixture of lime and mango juices, said to be rich in vitamins but sadly deficient in alcohol.

★

I had pushed the lentils round my plate, hidden some under the untouched couscous, and, in describing the repast as 'delicious', committed perjury. Now we were about to get what we'd come for – Tony Thrale's reminiscences of swinging Perivale. 'Jo was very beautiful. Clear blue eyes and a lot of blonde curls.'

'With flowers in them?' I remembered the photograph.

'Flowers in them quite often.'

'And her husband?'

'He was a surprise. I could never quite make out why she'd married him. He was very good looking, of course, and I think they'd been childhood sweethearts. She was the girl next door to his parents' house in Perivale. They went to school together, he carried her books, all that sort of that sort of thing . . .'

'Did you get to know him?'

'Hardly at all.'

'What was his job?'

'Something in the building trade – I believe he did rather well. Moved off the sites and into the office. She said he practically ran the business.'

I remembered the statements of the semi-detached neighbours. At about the time Jo vanished, her husband had got in building materials. They heard sounds at night and he explained he was dealing with a damp wall in the kitchen.

'Did they go out together?'

'Never. So far as I remember. I think she said he was seriously religious and spent a lot of his spare time doing things for a particular church. He wouldn't have enjoyed the Karma Club, or The Age of Aquarius in Alperton. That's where the cool people went.'

'Was it cool for you,' I wondered, 'being an articled clerk in a solicitors' office?'

'I wrote a column for an underground magazine. It was called "Kill All Lawyers". I showed it round the Aquarius so I kept my credibility.'

'What did your law firm think about that?'

'It was printed in green ink on green paper, so it was more or less illegible. Anyway, I don't think the partners subscribed to *Peeping Tom*.'

'Did the Twinehams quarrel about her going out, do you remember?'

'I'm not sure she told him everything. I mean, she always said she loved him and it would have been hard for anyone not to love her. I don't think she told him about all the clubs and bars we went to – she had some story about evening classes and study groups. Exams she had to prepare for. I got the feeling that he didn't ask too many questions, and our life was something she didn't take home with her.'

'*Your* life?' I asked him the question direct.

Tony Thrale smiled, less with embarrassment than a sort of pride. 'You know what we believed in then. "Make love not war."'

'Was war an available alternative?'

'Well, of course it wasn't. So we just made love.'

Glenda Thrale had been busy with a pouch and packet of cigarette papers. She had rolled a fairly fat cigarette which she now lit and inhaled deeply. Having got the thing alight, she handed it to her husband.

'You mean,' I thought this had to be asked, 'you and Josephine Twineham made love?'

'It's hard to describe her.' Tony Thrale was now drawing heavily on the joint, a habit which seemed to have a strong following among the over-fifties. 'When she walked into the club, or even if you bumped into her in the street, you'd feel somehow better, happier, more optimistic, as though the sun had just come out from behind a cloud and was shining brightly. She was beautiful, yes, and kind and interested in everybody. But it wasn't just that. She made people feel it was better to be alive.' He passed the joint back to his wife.

'She was a little tart.' Glenda, after inhaling again, came out with this verdict, a condemnation quite out of fashion in the sixties.

'She gave generously of herself.' Tony gently brought the language into the Age of Aquarius.

'Do you think Will Twineham ever found out, about you and Jo, I mean?'

'I don't think she ever told him. She didn't tell him everything.'

'Or very much. Could he have found out?'

'There was one time . . . I'd got an afternoon off. I can't remember why. And we went to the cinema together . . . What was the film? . . . *Blow up*. I'm sure I can remember. Well, we'd done pretty much everything you can do in the double seats at the back of the old Regal and we came out still interested in each other and we . . . well, we kissed. For a long time and pretty thoroughly. In the street. And then she said, "Don't look now". But I turned and saw her husband. He'd just walked out of a shop across the road. I'm not sure if he saw us. I don't think he did.'

At this point, Glenda handed me the wet-ended stub. Feeling that the information might peter out if I rejected it, I put the object between my lips, drew in a mouthful, choked slightly and blew two columns of smoke out of my nose, producing a small, mirthless laugh from Glenda. Tony took the dank object from me and handled it more expertly.

'Did she tell you if he ever tackled her about having seen you?'

'No. She'd left.'

'Left?'

'Shortly after that we heard she'd left him. No one ever knew where she'd gone.'

'Not with you?'

'I'm afraid not.'

'Or anyone else from the Age of Aquarius?'

'We were all mystified. There must have been someone else, we thought, someone we didn't know anything about.'

'Now you know what happened.'

'Of course. He killed her, didn't he? Will murdered her.'

'Is that what you think?'

'Don't you? Who else did they dig up, if he didn't?'

'I don't know.'

There was a silence then. No one spoke and the tape on the sound system was over. All the trappings of the past, the incense and the dope, the voices of Glenda's favourites, the Incredible String Band and Van Morrison (she had announced the performers' names as the music changed) had died away. Tony gave a little shiver, as though shaking off the past and doing his best to face the realities of the present.

'Of course,' he said firmly, 'there's no way you'll get me to come to Court to tell them any of this.'

'We realize that, Tony.' Bonny Bernard was conciliatory. 'This is mere background information. That's all Mr Rumpole wanted from you.'

'It doesn't help you anyway, does it?' Tony was looking at me. He was a man making, in a determined fashion, for the way out. 'I mean, the fact she had other lovers would only give him a motive for . . . doing what he did.'

'You think so?'

'Isn't it obvious?'

And isn't it obvious, I might have added, that you, Tony Thrale, ex-swinger and survivor from the Age of Aquarius, might have been, partly at least, the cause of her death. Instead I thanked him. 'You've been a great help, telling us about Jo. One more thing – how was her health?'

'She had enormous energy.'

'Never ill?'

'She did acid, of course. Acid was what we did then. Gave her some funny dreams at times, she told me.'

'No other problems?'

'She got breathless sometimes. She became quite faint, as though she couldn't breathe. I thought it was the way she lived. Trying to cram everything in while there was still time.'

'Did she go to a doctor? About the breathlessness, I mean?'

'I think she did once. She told me something about an enlarged muscle to her heart.' He smiled. 'I told her her heart was absolutely perfect.'

'Did she get any treatment?'

'I think she forgot about it. That would have been her way.'

Not long after that, Bernard and I were out in the street, breathing in air free from incense and the smell of exotic cheroots. I asked my solicitor to find out who Jo Twineham's doctor was and see if any notes survived.

'I'm afraid they weren't much help.' Bernard was apologetic.

'Well, at least we know a good deal more about the Twinehams.'

'None of it's much help to the defence, is it? You've got to admit that. All we know just explains why he did it.'

'I wouldn't agree with that . . . entirely. Oh, and if we have to meet Tony again, let's do it in Pommeroy's, shall we? At least somewhere he's living in the present.'

On my way into Chambers a few days later, I stopped at Cameras R Us and took delivery of several copies of the photograph Owen Oswald, the helpful ex-drummer, had thoughtfully sent me.

'Who was that group, the Pithead Stompers?' the girl who slid the vital evidence into a large envelope asked me. 'I've never heard of them.'

'No,' I told her, 'I don't imagine many people have. But they will now.'

I was at my desk in the smoke-free zone, idly turning the pages of Ackerman's *Forensic Medicine* to check on what the Master of the Morgues had to say on the information available from skeletons, when Soapy Sam again intruded on my life.

'Rumpole,' he said, 'I've been thinking about that case of yours. The chap who buried his wife under the floorboards.'

'Who is alleged to have buried her. We haven't had the trial yet.'

'I did offer to lead you in that case, Rumpole.'

'I thought I said "Thanks, but no thanks".'

'Of course, I would have done my best for your client.'

I didn't tell him what I thought of his best. Instead I raised a more immediate subject. 'Ballard, you and I have a vital matter to discuss.'

'But I have come to the conclusion not to take a brief in *R. v. Twineham*,' Ballard ploughed on. 'Your man has no possible defence.'

'This is a formal request to you, Ballard, to return my room to its status as a refuge for the peaceful enjoyment of a small cigar.'

'Rumpole, neither of us has anything to gain by taking up impossible causes.'

'I don't regard my cause as impossible. I understand you may have certain formalities to go through. Chambers meetings, getting the formal agreement of such puritanical spirits as Mizz Liz Probert, so I'll give you – well let's say three weeks. But you can do it, Ballard. You're entitled to do it as Head of Chambers. And I have to give you fair warning. If I'm still smoking in the street by the end of the month, the consequences to you may be dire.'

'Rumpole, I have absolutely no idea what you mean.'

It was the moment to produce Exhibit A, the prosecution's trump card. I produced it, handing a copy to the accused.

There was a silence during which I took Soapy Sam to be slowly appreciating the damning nature of the evidence. When he spoke, it was, I have to admit, with considerable self-control.

'That's me at Uni,' is what he said.

'True,' I told him. 'That central figure with its hair down to the shoulders, holding a guitar in a horribly suggestive fashion, is indeed you, Bonzo Ballard.'

The man attempted a brave smile and merely said, 'Fancy you having that.'

'A present from a well-wisher,' I told him. 'Look at the drummer.'

'Owen Oswald gave it to you?'

'Indeed he did.'

Rising from his seat, Ballard said, 'May I keep it?'

'Do what you like with it. Burn it. Tear it into small pieces and flush it down the clerks' room facility. I have copies. And one goes up on the Chambers notice-board if my reasonable request isn't granted by the end of the month.'

Ballard was on his way out, looking at the photograph and smiling, as I thought, bravely.

'The old Pithead Stompers,' he was muttering. 'How young we were then. How terribly young!'

Then he was gone, and I couldn't help feeling a moment's pity for the chap. I stifled the feeling. There is a tide in the affairs of men when you have to be completely ruthless.

The approach of a serious criminal trial has different effects on customers who are about to step into the dock, whose names appear in the title and who are to take on the starring role in the proceedings. Older pros, such as the senior members of the Timson clan, that famous family of South London villains, take such trials philosophically, as a necessary risk in the pursuit of a career. Younger suspects become cocky and show off, over-excited by their day in Court, and play the somewhat corny character study of a cheerful and, if possible, likeable cockney sparrow.

As his day in Court approached, Will Twineham seemed to withdraw into some inner life which had more significance for him than the prison interview room, the dock and the prospect of an unfriendly verdict. But he began to answer questions more sensibly, as though, in a detached sort of way, he was willing to help me through a difficult, if not impossible period of my life.

'It's kind of you. It's very kind of you to visit me.'

'Not kind at all. It's my job.'

'Kind of you. To take an interest.'

'I wanted to ask about your wife. Happy marriage, was it?'

'I was happy. I've never been happy since she . . . left me.'

'From her photograph . . . she must have been beautiful.'

'The photograph doesn't tell the whole story.'

'I just wonder. Did she go out much? I mean, was she at home in the evenings?'

'Sometimes she was – we lived our own lives, of course. I had the church and she was studying.'

'Studying what exactly?'

'She'd left school early and she wanted a degree in English. She went to classes. Discussion groups. She had friends in the discussion groups. I never begrudged her that.'

'Did you ever meet her friends?'

'I told you,' he looked only slightly impatient with my curiosity, 'she had her own life to lead. I never questioned her. She was as loving to me as ever she was. And we became closer, when she had her religious experience.'

'Religious?'

'She dreamed dreams and saw visions.'

'Visions?'

'She saw what I had only read about in our church. Visions that had never appeared to me. She saw the serpent and the four beasts full of eyes before and behind.'

I remembered the Age of Aquarius club and all that Tony Thrale had told me about the days of acid. Had a small tablet sent Jo off to join her husband in visions of strange phantoms and terrifying apparitions? They spoke of things I could never dream of, let alone understand . . . and I felt an intruder into the strange world inhabited by Will and Jo Twineham. But I had to go on looking for explanations.

'The bones under the floor. Are you telling us you don't know who was buried there?'

'Jo was.' He said it as casually as he had thanked me for visiting him.

'How do you know?'

'Because I buried her there.' I looked at Bernard, but he

avoided my gaze. We had travelled through the world of the serpents and the beasts full of eyes to something as flat and final as a plea of guilty to murder. We had lost our case, but I had to plod on, in search of further and better particulars.

'You'd better tell us about it.'

'I saw her. I came out of Gales . . . builders' suppliers in the High Street. I saw her outside the picture house.' And then he said quietly, in a matter-of-fact sort of way, 'A woman seated upon a scarlet-coloured beast, arrayed in purple, having a golden cup in her hand full of the abomination and filthiness of her fornication.'

I waited for the visions to fade, for my client to look hard at the cold interview room, the screw on the other side of the glass door, the dog handler in the prison yard under the window. Then I asked him the question he'd have to answer in Court. 'Mr Twineham, did you kill your wife?'

'Yes, I killed her.'

'And buried her body under the floor?'

'I buried her. Yes.'

'Because you were afraid of being charged with murder?'

He shook his head then and gave me one of his charming and disarming smiles. 'No. Because I didn't want to be parted from her.'

'Insanity's out.'

'You mean you've come to your senses, Rumpole, at last.'

Hilda made this critical observation in what was, for her, a relatively jovial manner, and I ignored it. I was getting outside a nourishing breakfast (egg, bacon and fried slice) before heading off to the Old Bailey for the case of Mr Twineham.

'He must have been sane, that's what all the quacks say, because he hid his wife's body. He knew perfectly well he'd committed a crime and was trying to escape detection. Even Bernard couldn't find a doctor who'd disagree with that. But in my view, burying your wife under the sitting-room floor is a sure sign of madness.'

'I should think so too.' She looked at me as though such an idea might never have entered my head. I changed the subject.

'By the way, how was the Old Girls' Reunion?'

'It went extremely well. In fact, it was a whole lot of fun. Dodo and I enjoyed it hugely.'

I tried to imagine what sort of fun the Old Saint Elfreda's Girls got up to, failed and said, 'But I thought you were dreading it?'

'Oh, we were.'

'How was Chrissie what's her name?'

'You mean Chrissie Snelling – Lady Shiplake now. She was in the chair.'

'And cut you two dead, did she?'

'Not at all. She was enormously pleased to see us. She kept saying what an entertaining pair we were at school. She said we were a laugh a minute.'

'She said that?' I tried to picture She Who Must and her friend Dodo Mackintosh as two capering schoolgirls constantly telling jokes and irritating the science mistress, but failed. 'But you said she left because of you and Dodo?'

'Oh, she explained that. It was nothing to do with us.'

'It wasn't?'

'No. Chrissie's father . . .'

'Snelling?'

'Yes. Anyway, he was high up in the Foreign Office and he got posted to Washington, so they decided to send her to school over there. It was quite a sudden decision.'

'And no one told you that . . . ?'

'No one.'

'So you've felt guilty. All these years?'

'Up till last night. Yes. As I said to Dodo, it's quite a weight off my mind.'

'It must be.' Did I see, I wondered, some faint glow of light at the end of Will Twineham's tunnel? A life spent in the mistaken assumption of guilt? Still chewing the last bit of breakfast, I set off to meet my client down the Bailey.

'Professor Ackerman, you can learn a good deal from a skeleton, can't you?'

'I can tell you that it was the skeleton of a fully grown woman approximately five foot four inches high. I would say the body had been buried carefully and the digger brought it up all in one piece.'

'Been buried carefully, had it?' Judge Cameron Foulks was a ginger-moustached, wary-eyed Scot who behaved, throughout his trials, in a military fashion, having a tendency to bark out orders as though without them courtroom discipline couldn't be maintained and proceedings might, at any moment, slide into anarchy. 'The Jury will remember that. A woman of average height, buried carefully.' So far the evidence was giving him great pleasure.

'Could you form any view as to how long ago the body was buried?' I asked the Master of the Morgues.

'A considerable time. More than twenty years.'

'It was thirty-three years ago that your client's wife disappeared.' The Judge was sitting bolt upright, perky as a cock who has just exercised his *droit de seigneur* over all the surrounding hens.

57

'I think the Jury can work that out without any assistance from your Lordship.' I thought the time had come to take the Judge down a peg or two. He considered flying at me in a whirl of ruffled feathers but, thinking better of it, relapsed into a sulky silence.

'Professor Ackerman, you're familiar with a condition known as obstructive cardiac myopathy.' Here I smiled at the Judge in a pleasant sort of way. 'May I spell that for your Lordship?' And before he could protest, I did so.

Then I turned from him to the witness.

'Is that a hardening of a muscle of the heart?'

'It is more or less that.'

'Doesn't it cause breathlessness and, in an extreme attack, death?'

'It could do, certainly.'

'And could such an attack be brought on by extreme emotional stress – in a young woman, for example?'

'I believe it might.'

'And if this young woman were taking drugs in the shape of LSD tablets, might that worsen her condition?'

'I don't think it would do her any good.'

'Mr Rumpole. Are you suggesting that death in this case had something to do with a heart condition?'

Prof. Ackerman and I had built up a certain rapport across many courts and in many murder trials. We both looked at the Judge who had interrupted our dialogue with a sort of weary patience.

'I congratulate your Lordship.' I smiled at him in a way he clearly found irritating. 'Your Lordship has grasped the exact nature of the defence.'

Before his Lordship could find the breath to reply, I asked the expert witness the next question.

'Was it possible to tell, from your examination of her bones, if this woman had any such heart condition?'

I knew, of course, what his answer was going to be, but Dr Paul of Acton was dead and his notes gone, God knows where. Asking my old friend and sparring partner, Professor Ackerman of the Morgues, the above question was the only way I had of getting the facts of this complaint in front of the Jury.

'I'm afraid, Mr Rumpole, I couldn't tell that.'

'He couldn't possibly tell that.' The Judge had his tail feathers up again. 'You've got your answer, Mr Rumpole.'

'Certainly I have, my Lord.' I continued to look as though it were just the answer I wanted. Then I changed the subject.

'Professor Ackerman, I want to ask you about the cause of death. Can you help us?'

'I'll do my best.'

'I'm sure you will. The skull was completely intact, wasn't it?'

'It was.'

'So we can rule out a heavy blow to the head, let us say with a blunt instrument?'

'Yes we can.'

'There were no broken bones?'

'There were not.'

'So we can rule out a violent attack?'

'I think so.'

'You mean very possibly we can rule such an attack out?'

'Yes.'

'There were no bones broken in the neck?'

'None.'

'So you can rule out violent strangulation?'

'There were no signs of violence on the skeleton. No.'

'So, to sum up, Professor. There was no evidence to show that this young woman had been murdered?'

The Court was silent, the Jury attentive as he answered fairly, 'No evidence from the bones I examined. No.'

'You did wonders with the Professor.'

'Thank you, Bernard. I made bricks without straw. What can we do with bones? They don't prove much. One way or the other.'

The prosecution had closed its case, and the steak and kidney and nourishing Guinness in the pub opposite the Old Bailey were to give me strength for what was likely to prove one of the trickiest afternoons in the Rumpole career. When our client admitted, calmly and as though it was the most natural thing in the world, that he killed his wife, Bernard was convinced there was no alternative to a guilty plea and told the Court as much. But things began to happen. Tony Thrale, perhaps ashamed of his determination to keep out of Court, remembered a couple of middle-aged ex-flower-power children who could speak of Jo's quest for adventure by way of acid tablets and the Age of Aquarius club. One of them even remembered an attack of breathlessness. I had talked to Will Twineham in the cells under the Old Bailey, and I believed he was in a fit state to enter the witness box.

It started well. Will stood, quiet, grey haired, good looking, in the dock. We went through his life as a young builder falling in love with the girl next door. We got through his promotion to management, his married life and Jo's frequent absences. He remained calm as he described the lengthy kiss he saw in front of the cinema.

'I waited for her to come home. It seemed that I went on a journey.'

'You mean you left the house?'

'Not in the body. In the spirit.'

'In the body you stayed waiting for her?'

'Yes. But my spirit was upon the side of the sea.'

Poor old His Lordship looked thoroughly confused. 'Is your client saying he went to the seaside, Mr Rumpole?'

'His spirit went, my Lord.'

'I'm not interested in where his spirit went to.'

'He went to the seaside, only in his imagination, my Lord.'

'Mr Rumpole. Whatever is in his imagination is not evidence. You should know better by now. Considering the length of time you've been at the Bar.'

I decided to ignore such rudeness and turned to the witness. 'Mr Twineham. Tell the Court. What did you do?'

'I saw a beast rising out of the sea,' Will told the Judge in the most matter-of-fact tone of voice, 'having seven heads and ten horns, and upon his horns, ten crowns and upon his heads the name of blasphemy.'

'Mr Rumpole.' The Judge was getting desperate. 'Has this beast, whatever it is, anything at all to do with your case?'

'Not directly, my Lord,' I had to admit.

'Then get the beast out of my Court. Can't you persuade your client to give evidence in the proper manner?'

'I'll try. Mr Twineham, did your wife come home?'

'She came home later.'

'What did you do?'

'I told her what I had seen. Coming out of Gales, I had seen her with a man, kissing, in the way of fornicators.'

'Did she deny it?'

'No. She laughed. It was one of the moods she had. When she came home. Laughing. But then she stopped laughing.'

'What did you do?'

'I believe I killed her.'

It was what we had all come there to decide, but suddenly, unexpectedly, the decision seemed to have been made. The Jury looked away, as if embarrassed by the moment of truth, this stark admission. I had to show them that it wasn't at all as simple as that.

'You say you *believe* you killed her?'

'I believe that, yes.'

'Did you strike her over the head?'

'I never did that.'

'Did you strangle her?'

'I didn't do that either.'

'Did you have your hands round her throat?'

'Never.'

'Did you touch her at all?'

'I never touched her.' Will Twineham seemed surprised by his own answer.

'But you say you believed you killed her?'

'I shouted at her. I called out in a loud voice.'

'What did you call out?'

'I told her. I told her what I could see when I looked at her.'

'What was that?'

'A woman. Arrayed in purple, having a cup in her hand full of abominations and filthiness of fornications. I believe I called her the great mother of harlots and abominations of the Earth . . .'

'What happened then . . . ?'

'The words killed her.'

'The words?'

'She was upset. I could see that. As if she couldn't breathe. She was fighting for breath. I saw that. I saw her fall . . . She never got up again.'

'And you swear you never touched her?'

'Never! It was the words. The power of the words was too much for her strength.'

'And then?'

'Then I did touch her. There was no heart. No breath either. I watched by her all night. All next day too. And the next night, when I was sure she was dead, I buried her.'

'Where?'

'In front of the fireplace. Under the big hearthstone. I knew the earth was soft there. I laid her gently . . . And then I covered her over.'

The Jury were watching him now, puzzled by a scene they could hardly imagine, let alone understand.

'Did you do that because you were afraid you'd be accused of murdering her?'

'No.'

'Why then?'

'I loved her.' He was looking at the Jury now. 'I wanted to keep her with me.' It was what he had always told us.

Two days later, I was waiting for the Jury to come back with a verdict. The trial had gone as smoothly as possible. Old George Kilroy for the prosecution had asked Will, over and over again, about his lies to the neighbours and the story that Jo had left him. To all of which Will smiled and said that she had left him by dying, and he had wanted, above all, to keep her close to him. The Judge, who would never, so long as he lived, be able to dream dreams and see visions, had told the

Jury that there was only one reason for Jo's burial in the house. Will Twineham wanted to avoid the inevitable justice which had been so long delayed.

'Will your foreman please stand?'

A grey-haired woman rose to her feet. I had counted her as a friend in the Jury. She had listened intently and smiled at my occasional jokes.

'Have you reached a verdict on which you are all agreed?'

'We have.'

'Do you find the defendant, William Twineham, guilty or not guilty of murder?'

She was looking straight at Will, neither apologetic nor embarrassed, which is always meant to be a good sign. My hopes soared until she spoke.

'Guilty.'

When I went down to the cells with Bernard, I had the sour taste of failure in my mouth and he said nothing to console me except words as trite as 'You can't win them all, Mr Rumpole.' Of course I started every case, however unpromising, hoping to win some small victory, and no loss was ever welcome. But now something worse seemed to have happened: the old Bailey, dedicated to common sense and hard facts, had failed in an act of the imagination. The life of the Twinehams had remained a mystery and Justice had not been done. These were my thoughts as we passed the carefully preserved door of the old Newgate prison, blacked with age and scarred with initials of hopeless cases on their way to the gallows. We saw the bulky screws brewing up tea and eating doorstep sandwiches and one of them called out, 'He's waiting for you, Mr Rumpole.'

And there he was, out of his cell and in the cramped

interview room, waiting patiently, as he would wait to see if he could live out his life sentence, and, incredibly, smiling.

'I want to thank you, Mr Rumpole,' he said. 'For all you've done. I honestly believe it's what I wanted.'

'You wanted to spend your old age in prison?'

'It's fair and right. Seems to me. I closed her up. I did that to her. I put earth and cement on her and shut her away. It's right I should be shut away too. Shut away from the world as she was. Like this, it seems to me now, we're still together. You can't understand that, can you?'

Will Twineham had been right. I couldn't understand it. There had been, in a destroyed semi-detached near Hangar Lane, a clash between two worlds, both alien to me. The Book of Revelations had met the Age of Aquarius, fallen in love and reached a conclusion which involved death, the concealment of a young body until it became, over the years, a collection of bones for a forensic expert to pick over. As I walked back to our Chambers, I knew the case, which had filled the last few days, would never vanish from my mind. It would remain a nagging doubt, perhaps, a recollection of failure to return in black moments. But its place would be taken by simpler, more ordinary cases and, above all, by the great case in which I felt sure of success – *Rumpole* v. *Soapy Sam Ballard*. Remembering this, a spring came into the Rumpole step and I bore down on Equity Court to taste the fruits of victory.

On my way to my room, I passed the Chambers notice-board – the place where I had threatened to pin up the cherished picture of the Pithead Stompers. And then I stopped dead in my tracks. The photograph was already there. High above the government health warnings and the list of

services in Temple Church, there was the band and Bonzo
Ballard strutting his stuff, grinning inanely with long hair
flopping to his shoulders and an electric guitar, a monstrous
instrument, apparently erupting from his crotch. The familiar
voice of Mizz Liz Probert was heard from behind me.

'Haven't you seen it before, Rumpole? Isn't it cool?'

'Who put it there?'

'Ballard did. He showed it to us at the last Chambers
meeting. When you were busy with that poor buried woman.
We thought it was great.'

'*Great?* What do you mean, great?'

'Well, we always thought he was a bit stuffy. You know,
rather dull. But now we know. He had a life once. Good on
Ballard, that's what I say. We thought it right to go up on the
notice-board.'

She looked at me in a critical sort of way. 'You were never
part of a group, were you, Rumpole?'

'Never,' I assured her. 'Never at any time. I'm a one-off.
Entirely on my own.' Which is exactly how I felt as I made
my way to my room in the smoke-free zone.

There was tentative sunlight in Equity Court, and the falling
drops of water from the fountain were coloured by it. Snow-
drops and early daffodils were out in the Temple gardens.
The scent of spring was nicely qualified by the smell of the
small cheroot I was still obliged to smoke alfresco. I hadn't
the heart to pursue Bonzo Ballard further – for the moment.
He had behaved, I have to admit, with totally unexpected
craftiness and some degree of courage. He had outsmarted
me and I had to hand it to him. The day of reckoning would
come, but perhaps not yet. The sour taste of a guilty verdict
had passed. I had been tempted, perhaps for a dark moment,

to hang up my wig, refuse all further work and await death in some dark corner of Pommeroy's Wine Bar, spinning out my half-bottle of Château Fleet Street and failing to finish the crossword. No longer. Spring had brought me an affray at Snaresbrook and I had thought of an ingenious defence. Rumpole was himself again.

Rumpole and the Asylum Seekers

It was about dawn on a bitterly cold April morning, with snow flurries and freezing fog, when a lorry, loaded with crates of imported mango chutney, was stopped in Dover Harbour. Men in bright-yellow jackets, inspecting the cargo, became suspicious at what appeared to be breathing holes in one of the crates. There was also a curious knocking as though some of the chutney was anxious to escape. Further investigation revealed the true nature of the cargo: not pickle but ten refugees from Afghanistan, men, women and three children. As they were liberated and lined up beside the lorry, an enterprising newsman got a picture of them which appeared, in blurred colour, on the front page of Hilda's tabloid under the headline 'BRITAIN REPELS MANGO CHUTNEY INVADERS'.

'When will it end, Rumpole?' Hilda gazed into an uneasy future. 'Soon we won't be able to tell Gloucester Road from Suez High Street.'

'These are Afghans,' I tried to explain. 'I don't suppose they've been anywhere near Suez High Street, wherever that may be. What puzzles me is why on earth they want to come here.'

'Why on earth shouldn't they? It's Britain.' Hilda turned to a page headed 'FAMOUS BOTTOMS. FIT THESE TO THE

FACES OF THE STARS', which she proceeded to study with great interest.

'I mean spring has become indistinguishable from mid-winter. The Tube broke down last night and we spent an hour trapped between the Temple and Embarkment. All the animals have apparently got infectious diseases and the countryside is lit with funeral pyres. Get a bit ill and you're sentenced to forty-eight hours on a trolley. I'm surprised that anyone would take the trouble of creeping into the country disguised as some sort of exotic condiment.'

'Rumpole! You're just trying to be irritating!'

There was some truth in this accusation, but having found a theme I was loath to abandon it. 'Anyway, why are they called "asylum seekers"? They used to be called refugees, which meant they were looking for a refuge from persecution. "Asylum seekers" means they're looking for a madhouse, which given the present state of the country might be an accurate description.' I had worked myself into a state of gloom, and I was quite enjoying it.

'What you want, Rumpole,' Hilda had moved on to the 'Home and Style' pages of her paper, 'is a complete makeover.'

'A what?'

'A re-think. An adjustment to an entirely fresh concept. Like this flat.'

'This flat? What's wrong with this flat?'

I looked round our home, the mansion flat that is decidedly not a mansion. It has, however, the virtues of familiarity. The sitting-room carpet may have become a little worn, a little marked round the fireplace by the stubs of inaccurately thrown small cigars aimed for the grate, the chintz of the chair covers might have become a little faded, the cream paint less creamy, the wallpaper, to some extent, losing contact with the bathroom ceiling. But I liked the creaky reception of the sofa, and the shelves of read and re-read books. Even Dodo Mackintosh's water-colours depicting Lamorna Cove in doubtful weather had reached the status of old friends. As with my gown, which was ever in danger of coming apart at the seams, and my wig, which has long since lost its whiteness and achieved the respectably yellowish tinge of old parchment, I had grown contented with the appearance of the mansion flat which, when not blasted with the cold winds of Hilda's displeasure, was a perfectly comfortable place to inhabit.

'Something is happening out there, Rumpole. There's no reason why this flat shouldn't be part of it.'

'Something? You mean some sort of demonstration? You want our flat to leave home and join in?' I might have said that but, no doubt wisely, I thought better of it. 'I've got to get to work,' I told her.

'That's your answer to everything, isn't it, Rumpole? Work. It stops you thinking about how we're going to keep up with the times.'

As usual, I thought, as I embarked on the journey from Gloucester Road Tube station, which had become about as complex and unpredictable as the Road to Mandalay, Hilda was perfectly right.

Among the refugees from Afghanistan was Doctor Mohammed Nabi, trained and qualified during happier moments in the history of his country. When a new regime took over he had paid a large sum for his trip in the chutney wagon. Having sold all he possessed and borrowed a thousand dollars from relatives and well-wishers, he found his country as easy to escape from as England was hard to get into.

After his emergence from the crate, the lengthy process began. The Doctor and his companions were sent to a vacant council house on the outskirts of a town in Kent, where he was given vouchers to buy a minimum amount of food. There he was allowed ten days to fill in a nineteen-page form in English. The form was sent off to the Home Office, who undertook to give no answer unless it was a rejection. In due course the rejection arrived. This refusal led me into a hitherto unknown field and to invest in a slim publication, designed for students, called *All You Need to Know about Immigration Law*.

'Civil Rights. Freedom of the Individual. Defeat for the Forces of Darkness. That's what you stand for, don't you, Mr Rumpole?'

Mr Minter, 'Call me Ted', was a large, untidy, perpetually smiling man with the look of an astute rabbit. His upper lip a little raised, he spoke with a slight lisp. He was, he told me, 'Old Labour' so far as his political beliefs went, which meant that he had an unfashionable faith in such concepts as the Rights of Man. He carried on a practice outside Canterbury, and undertook Legal-Aid cases for those in flight from foreign tyrannies. He carried a bulging briefcase and had two holes in the sweater he wore under a crumpled tweed suit.

'I'm a newcomer to this branch of the law,' I told him. 'What on earth made you choose me?'

'We knew you'd have the right attitude, Mr Rumpole. Men like the good Doctor come here and everyone's against them. The government, the opposition, most of the public and the newspapers. You speak up for them.'

'Only to my wife,' I had to tell him, and perhaps that

was only for the entirely legitimate purpose of starting an argument. 'I have to confess I never did one of these difficult cases.'

'But you've won enough difficult cases, Mr Rumpole, we know that.'

'We? Who's we?'

'Well, I know and the client does.'

'You mean this Doctor Nabi?'

Ted made a quick search of his briefcase, as though unsure which of his many customers we were concerned with, pulled out a sheet of paper and looked at it with some relief. 'That's the one! I have his notes here. He asked for you specifically. Your fame has gone before you, Mr Rumpole.'

In my imagination I crossed the snows of high mountains to swoop down on a crowded market square, loud with the squawk of chickens and the braying of donkeys, filled with brown-eyed men in turbans whispering to each other, 'If you're ever in trouble, send for Rumpole!'

'My fame – even in Afghanistan?'

'Apparently.'

'Likeable fellow, this Doctor, is he?' I had already formed a favourable opinion of the man.

'I don't know.'

'You don't?'

'The fact is,' Ted the solicitor looked embarrassed, 'I've never seen him.'

'What?'

'It seems he's afraid of something, or someone. He says his life's threatened – I'm not sure who by exactly. I get my instructions through a friend.'

'A friend of yours?'

'A friend of his. Another Afghan called Jamil. He seems to

be a sort of social worker who gives advice to asylum seekers. He helps them fill in their forms. He does all that for the Doctor.'

'And the Doctor doesn't speak to you?'

'I'm not quite clear why. Jamil says he's in a state of depression since his application was turned down. He needs all our help, Mr Rumpole . . .'

'I'll have to see him before the hearing.' I was now becoming impatient with this arm's-length client, apparently determined to keep his distance.

'Oh, you will see him. You'll certainly see him. Meanwhile . . .' Ted dug into his briefcase and brought up a great wodge of paper, flimsy copies of forms filled in, formal rejections and tales of a political regime that beggared belief.

'They all say you're a legend in your lifetime, Rumpole. Your fame's spread far and wide.'

The man who paid me this apparent compliment was small, dressed in a dapper suit, with shoes so brightly polished you might see your face in them. He had light-brown hair, which stood up on either side of a bald patch, and the face of an immoderately self-satisfied Pekinese. Did I detect in his elaborate compliment a note of sarcasm? If so, I ignored it and gave him the facts.

'I am quite well known, it seems,' I said, 'in Afghanistan.'

'Isn't that where they make you grow beards, Rumpole? I say, wouldn't Rumpole look splendid with a bloody great beard down to his navel? Don't you all think Rumpole would make a splendid Ayatollah?'

This man had been introduced to me as Archie Prosser, known, Erskine-Brown told me, as the 'Boy Wonder' at Winchester. He had a good mixed practice, Claude also said, and was looking for new Chambers. As Archie spoke, he gave a little wriggle of delight, deeply enjoying his own jokes. In my opinion, they weren't worth the wriggle, although they were greeted with loud laughter by the assembled company in Pommeroy's Wine Bar. Claude was there, of course, and Mizz Liz Probert and Hoskins, who laughed so immoderately at the idea of a bearded Rumpole that his usual anxiety about the expense of rearing his daughters seemed forgotten.

Ballard, who since his revelation as the one-time Bonzo, lead singer of the Pithead Stompers, had taken to joining the tenantry in Pommeroy's, where he sat smiling and indulging himself in a potent mixture of orange juice and lemonade, also laughed heartily.

'It's got nothing to do with beards.' I was, I confess, rather short with them all. 'It's an Afghan doctor, who chose me to represent him.'

'What's he done? Medical negligence or indecent assault?'

'Neither. He just wants to live in England. Eccentric of him, you may say, but that's what he wants.'

'They come here,' Archie Prosser looked serious, 'because we're an easy touch.'

'Not all that easy. He's had all his applications refused so far.'

'Quite right.' Prosser's Pekinese face took on an expression of high judicial authority. 'These people need cracking down on.'

'Cracking down?' I felt strongly on this subject. 'We always seem to be cracking down on everyone – one-parent families, lawyers, windscreen washers, refugees and those who like an occasional small cheroot!' Here I flattened Bonzo Ballard with a stare. 'Why don't we try cracking up something for a change, such as the great British tradition of welcoming political refugees?'

Unlike the Boy Wonder's jokes, this speech was greeted with an embarrassed silence by the assembled members of 1 Equity Court. They appeared to cheer up slightly when the entertaining Archie said, 'I heard about your smoking habit, Rumpole. I heard you rather enjoy standing out of doors chatting up the secretaries in all sorts of weather.'

When the totally uncalled-for, and I thought somewhat forced, laughter subsided, Ballard, proving that 'Soapy Sam' was, indeed, an apt description, said, 'I'm so glad we brought you two together, Rumpole. I knew you'd find Prosser a kindred spirit, and a great asset to Chambers.' It was a statement which I thought called for a firm 'No comment.'

'It'll be a joy to share with Rumpole, well known as the Chambers wit and the joker in the pack. Come to think of it,' the Boy Wonder stared at me and gave a little preparatory wriggle before what he clearly considered would be a sure-fire hit, 'you haven't said anything funny the whole evening.'

When troubles come, they come not single spies, or even single asylum seekers. Finding that the company in Pommeroy's seriously detracted from the pleasure of the Château Thames Embankment, I arrived home early to find the usually quiet and uneventful flat in Froxbury Mansions positively buzzing with activity. Hilda was not alone, but in the company of a couple who looked, at first sight, inexplicable. They were not people she could possibly have been at school with, or even met at bridge. For a moment, I thought they must be refugees come to consult me owing to my spreading fame in such cases. Were they perhaps young members of a resistance group subject to persecution, and perhaps torture, in their native land? They looked pale and deeply serious, with the manner of fervent believers in some cause, and the young man, his head shaven to premature baldness, wore the trousers of some military force with huge pockets at the knees, perhaps for the storing of hand grenades. Above them, he wore a puffed-up waistcoat which might be useful for keeping afloat after your plane ditched in the water. The girl, who had long, straight hair and small spectacles, clearly had some trouble securing her jeans – the top fly-buttons were undone, causing them to slip below her hips exposing the dingy tops of a pair of knickers and an expanse of pale stomach before the advent of a faded T-shirt which bore the legend ACTIV8 YOURSELF. The message seemed to have gone unattended because she stood leaning against a wall, her glasses on the end of her nose and her eyes closed in evident exhaustion, while her male companion was busy with a metal tape, apparently measuring us up. As I stood looking at the couple with wild surmise, the young man asked me if I'd mind shifting so he could measure the distance from the door to the gas fire.

'There's plenty of room,' he said with satisfaction, 'for the talk pit.'

'When we take away the gas fire and those absolutely ghastly tiles, and the mantelpiece, of course, we're going to make this the "Relationship Area".' The girl unexpectedly spoke, and then refreshed herself from the large, plastic bottle of mineral water she carried with her.

'Hilda!' I heard in my voice bewilderment turning to desperation. 'Who are these people?'

'Mark and Sue,' she started to explain. 'From the television.'

'Surely we don't have to move the gas fire and the mantelpiece to accommodate the television. I mean, the television's there, on its stand, where it's always been. It doesn't take up much room.'

'Rumpole. Sue and Mark are from *Make Over*. We've been chosen as a London flat to be made over.'

'A gone-to-seed, deeply worn-out London flat.' Mark spoke with missionary enthusiasm. 'We're here to liberate it! To give it new life. To let it *breathe*, for once!'

'I'm not sure our flat is noticeably short of breath.'

'Aren't you? Well, just tell us – how's your relationship?' He looked from one to the other of us. The girl moved away from the wall, her eyes open. It was a question clearly of deep interest to both of them. Neither of us answered it.

Instead Hilda said, 'They're going to give us a talk pit.'

'A *what*?'

'It's a space you sit in. A sort of hole. Quite comfortable.'

'Like a grave?' I couldn't help myself.

'Sitting below floor level,' Mark explained, 'you'll find yourselves saying things to each other you never thought of saying before.'

'I should think we might. But you can't dig a hole in the middle of our sitting-room. You'd crash through Colonel Daventry's ceiling in number 31A and he'd be extremely angry.'

'No problems,' Mark said. 'Pas de probs.' To which he added, 'We're simply going to raise your floor three feet.

'We'll knock through that door and include the passage.'

'Get rid of all those horrible dangling lights and have lava lamps.'

'And as this is the Relationship Zone, we'll have shelves behind the talk pit to put the crystals on.'

'Crystals?' I was doing my best to keep up with the plans for our matrimonial home.

'We'll place a large crystal directly facing the talk pit,' Sue explained to me as though to a child, 'so it can really *help* with your relationship.'

The mind boggled at the idea of my long, sometimes stormy attachment to She Who Must Be Obeyed being seriously affected by a lump of glittering rock.

'We thought the walls dead white. Just blank pages, really. For your thoughts.'

'With lights so you can change wall colour according to your mood.'

'We find most couples turn on yellow for happiness and accord.'

'Scarlet for passion.'

And black, I thought, for complete matrimonial incompatibility. My reverie was interrupted by Hilda's curt 'Why don't you go into the kitchen, Rumpole, and read your *Evening Standard*, so Sue and Mark can get on with their job?'

As I left, I heard them discussing see-through storage drawers, so you could always see your underclothes.

Much later, Hilda joined me in the kitchen. 'What the hell,' I asked her, 'are lava lamps?'

'Beautiful things, Rumpole. Sort of tubes of light with bubbles running up and down. Like the stuff that comes out of volcanoes.'

'Lava?'

'Exactly!'

'All this redecoration,' I did my best to sound reasonable and keep the panic out of my voice, 'is out of the question. It'd cost us a fortune!'

'That's where you're wrong, Rumpole. It won't cost us a single penny.'

'Who's going to pay for it, then?'

'The television.'

'Hilda, please. Face up to reality.'

'I am. Have you never seen the *Make Over* programme? No? You've always been asleep, or reading about some dreadful crime or other. The real world is passing you by. They take people's homes and make them over.'

'Make them over to what? The bankruptcy court?'

'Make them over to modern, lovable, hugely desirable residences where relationships can grow and flourish. And the television company pays.'

'But why us, Hilda? Why, out of the entire population, did they choose us?'

'I wrote, Rumpole. It was when I said that you needed a makeover that I got the idea. So I wrote to the programme and told them we had a typically seedy sort of London flat, and Mark and Sue came to see us and the answer was "Yes". They'll do a programme about us.'

'A programme?' The voice was faint, the mind had grown tired of boggling.

'Of course. They'll show the whole rebuilding thing and us as we enjoy our new lifestyle. You'll be on the television. You'll be famous, Rumpole.'

'You mean – the whole country will see us?'

'Yes, of course.' Hilda sounded delighted. 'Nationwide.'

'So Judge Bullingham and Soapy Sam Ballard and the Lord Chief Justice and the Commissioner of the Metropolitan Police – not to mention the Timsons and my next Jury and the entire population of Wormwood Scrubs – can watch me sitting with you in a talk pit having our relationship cemented by beams of light from crystal balls and volcanic eruptions? Do you honestly think, Hilda, that's going to be a great help to my practice at the criminal Bar?'

'Of course it will! You need a bit of publicity, Rumpole. No one's ever heard of you. Now you'll be quite famous. Oh, and I've got another piece of good news. I got a call from Elsie Prosser. Elsie Inglefield as was.'

'You mean,' I could sense what was coming, 'you two were at school together?'

'Of course we were. Elsie Inglefield was a house monitor with me at St Elfreda's. That was before she married the Honourable Archie Prosser.'

'The Boy Wonder? What's honourable about him?'

'He's Lord Binfield's son. And Elsie tells me he's joined your Chambers. A bit of a feather in the cap of 1 Equity Court, isn't it?'

'Hardly.'

'Anyway, I've invited them here to dinner. It's a long time ahead, but make a note in your diary. Of course we can tell them about it, but I'm afraid the new talk pit won't be ready by then.'

A pity, I thought. I could have pushed the Hon. Archie Prosser into it and nailed down the lid.

The neglected council house somewhere in Kent was a place that had no talk pit, no lava lamps and had never been subjected to any sort of makeover. The walls showed the damp, and hot water was a distant memory since the boiler packed up. The windows were frequently broken by local inhabitants, resentful of strangers whom they suspected were after their jobs or had come to sponge off their taxes. The men played cards or sometimes, in the evenings, sang national laments, or outdated rock numbers they had heard secretly on banned radios. The women, astonished at being allowed to uncover their faces or wear trousers without fear of the lash, giggled and gossiped in the kitchen. The children whooped with delight as they chased each other up and down the stairs, playing as they might have done in their villages or in the back streets of Kabul, only knowing they were out on an adventure and not caring where, or how, their future lives would be led. In one of the overcrowded bedrooms a man lay with his face to the wall, sunk in a deep depression and hopeless gloom. The others, as though afraid that this condition might be contagious, as far as possible avoided him.

When Ted Minter the solicitor called at this address, Doctor Mohammed Nabi was no longer there. He had stirred himself, gone out to buy a little food with his vouchers and not returned.

'I told you he's afraid for his life, Mr Rumpole. Maybe it's some of the other refugees. Perhaps it's part of the Mafia that smuggled him over.'

'Mafia?' I asked Ted to explain.

'The Russian Mafia. Aided by quite a few Afghans on the make. The mango chutney element has the stamp of Afghans on it.'

'So which of their organizations is threatening the Doctor?'

'Jamil doesn't know. He says the Doctor hasn't any idea, but it was a Russian he paid originally.'

'And the Doctor's vanished?'

'I told you, I only get instructions through Jamil.'

'And have you met this Jamil?'

'He telephones me.'

'So what organization does he belong to?'

'Well,' Ted became vague, started a search in his over-stuffed briefcase again and gave it up. 'As I said, he's some kind of social worker. They've certainly heard of him at the Asylum Seekers' Council. He keeps them informed. He speaks reasonable English, so he can cope with the forms. It's not entirely satisfactory.'

'If you want my honest legal opinion, it's bloody hopeless.'

'It was before the adjudicator.' Ted smiled as if the general hopelessness of the world he operated in caused him only vague amusement. 'Neither of them turned up, not Jamil, not the Doctor. My instructions were to go on without them. Read the statements, you know the sort of thing. Make the legal argument. Of course they threw us out. The strange thing was . . .'

'What?'

'We got leave to appeal to the Tribunal.'

'As a reward for not bothering to turn up?'

'I had to undertake to get the Doctor to the Appeal.'

'Sounds a pretty hopeless undertaking.'

'Jamil says the Doctor realizes it's vitally important. He'll be there. Another strange thing . . .'

'What?'

'They've made it a "Starred Appeal". As though we were going to decide some great point of legal principle.'

'Tell the Doctor's messenger that the vital point of legal principle is whether he bothers to turn up, not only to the hearing but to a conference in these Chambers within the next two weeks. And if he can't force himself to do that, you can send him a message of goodbye from Rumpole.'

'Rumpole, do you know the one about marriage being like a hurricane?'

'Yes,' I told the Boy Wonder, but it didn't deter him in the least.

'It starts with all that sucking and blowing and you end up by losing your house!' Our addition to Equity Court then laughed immoderately. Having heard this joke told somewhat better by Jack Pommeroy the week before, I gave a weakish smile.

'You don't know many jokes, do you, Rumpole?'

'Only one,' I had to confess, 'and that's not a true belly laugh.'

'Tell us though.'

The fact that you've been offered a seat in Chambers, was what I'd intended to say, but I decided not to bring myself down to the Archie Prosser level. Instead I told him I had to get to the Temple station before they privatized the Underground and caused total chaos on the Circle Line.

To this he answered unexpectedly, 'You know we have girls in the Sheridan Club now?'

'No, I didn't know.'

'A lot of the members were against it, but I like to see a girl round the old place occasionally. Cheers a fellow up.'

'Does it really?'

'So what I meant to say was, could you stop in for a drink at the old place? There's a girl member there longing to meet you. Bunty Heygate. You've heard of her, of course – a real live wire of the Home Office team.'

A live wire at the Home Office sounded a bit of an oxymoron, like hot ice. That gloomy institution, dedicated to cracking down on Magna Carta, the Presumption of Innocence, the right to cross-examine or any other available aid to a fair trial, seemed to me to be shrouded in perpetual darkness. 'But why ever,' I asked Archie, 'does this Home Office luminary want to see me?'

'Afghanistan.'

'Oh yes?' For once the fellow was beginning to hold my attention.

'Aren't you defending some doctor who came in with a load of pickles?'

'Something like that.'

'Over here no doubt to sponge on our National Health Service.'

'You mean there's a terrible danger he might help get a few patients off their trolleys?'

'Come and meet Bunty anyway.' Archie was in no way put out. 'She's heard such a lot about you. Oh, and by the way, see if you can't think of a few jokes.'

'A drink in the Sheridan Club with the Honourable Archie Prosser and the star of the Home Office, Rumpole? Of course you've got to go. And remind him about coming here on the fourteenth of the month after next. It seems Archie is tied up for dinner till then.'

'Tied up for dinner.' I thought about it as Archie raised a glass of champagne to his lips. Was he frequently tied up, trussed, roasted to a pleasant, light brown and served, perhaps with an orange in his mouth, on a silver platter? My dream was interrupted by a throaty female voice calling, 'Cheers, Mr Rumpole.' She drank and, without hesitation, I followed her example.

I had come, at Hilda's express order, to the Sheridan Club, hidden in the purlieus of Whitehall. The room we sat in was large and gloomy, lit by a single chandelier, with chocolate-brown walls and furnished with armchairs flattened by long use in the seating department and shiny, like jackets worn at the elbows. The temperature in the room was a good four degrees lower than the outside air, so chilling the champagne seemed unnecessary.

This was the institution to which women had, after a long campaign against a determined opposition, gained access, an event greeted by the papers as though it were as great an historical moment as entry to the House of Commons or the priesthood. Some of these 'girls' were dotted about the room. Grey-haired, darkly clothed, bespectacled, they were hard to distinguish from the elderly, pink-cheeked, high-voiced old men they were entertaining or being entertained by.

Bunty Heygate was an exception. She might well, with some justification, still have been called a 'girl'. Her blonde hair was cut in a fashionable page-boy manner. Her face was fresh and her eyes appealing. She wore a red coat and skirt with darker velvet at the collar and cuffs, and heels just this side of a fetishist's delight. Her voice had that note of command learned as part of the curriculum in girls' boarding schools.

'We so admire the way you stand up in Court, Mr Rumpole, fighting for human rights,' Bunty told me.

'Do you really?' This, from a member of the Government, was something of a revelation.

'I want you to believe we're right behind you.'

'So far behind that you're practically out of sight. Judging from what your Home Secretary said.'

'Mr Rumpole,' she interrupted me with a tolerant smile, 'we politicians have to live in the real world. I've got constituents in the North of England, men who gather in pubs and discuss hanging and flogging first-time offenders – that's after they've castrated them, of course. Now, when we make statements about our policy, those are the people we have to think about.'

'You mean the men in pubs?'

'Exactly! But we do respect what you said in Court about Jury trials . . .'

'Members of the Jury, you are the lamp that shows the light of freedom burns.' I had said that in a case at Snaresbrook concerning sending indecent magazines through the post. It got reported in the *Guardian* as a saying of the week, but the Jury convicted me. I was grateful to Bunty for remembering it. Then I asked, 'Why are you cutting down on Jury trials?'

'Mr Rumpole,' Bunty was smiling gently. 'Get real. Have you ever been north of Watford?'

'Very often. Have you?'

'I do try to go. But since I became a member here, it's so tempting to stay in London.' There was a pause as she looked round the room with apparent affection, at the dark walls, the wheezing chairs and the members' guests who were looking with awe at the central table set out with back numbers of *The Field* and *Country Life* and the portrait of Richard Brinsley Sheridan. He was looking down in some disapproval at the club which bore his name and yet seemed singularly short of drunken playwrights and loud-voiced, bosomy actresses. Bunty Heygate MP was examining her well-tended nails and she started almost shyly. 'You're representing Doctor Nabi, Archie told me.'

'I hope to be, when we can find him. I was told you think it's an important case. A Starred Appeal they said. That's very flattering.'

'The Foreign Office have taken a view, haven't they, Bunty?' Archie Prosser, who seemed to move in high political circles, was helping her out.

'Well, to be honest with you,' she smiled at me disarmingly, 'we have a problem. We do have to respect, well, other nations whose ways may be different from ours. We have to respect their ethnicity.'

'Ethnicity?' It was a word to which I had not yet become accustomed. 'What does that mean, exactly?'

'Well, you see, we want an Afghan to be proud of his Afghanism, his religion, his customs. His traditional way of life. It's not politically correct, we feel, for us to impose white, Western values on another civilization. We would not want Afghans . . .'

'To become members of the Sheridan Club, for instance?' I suggested. This appeared to irritate Bunty, who became noticeably less friendly.

'It's not like that! It's, well . . . As you know, they have their own ways of dealing with theft, which seem perfectly reasonable to them.'

'You mean by chopping off people's hands?'

'It's all part of their Sharia law.'

'Which would be extremely popular with those men in pubs up North you keep talking about. You know the Afghan police make their local doctors attend to the hand-chopping?' My cross-examiner's blood was up.

'There's no direct evidence of that.' Archie Prosser seemed to know.

'There will be! Once I get the good Doctor in front of the Tribunal.'

'All I'm trying to say, Mr Rumpole,' Bunty leaned forward and spoke now in a low, eager voice, almost as if she were making a declaration of love, 'is that this country has to maintain reasonably friendly relations with countries and people . . . all over the world.' Here she spread out her hands as though to embrace Mormons, Seventh Day Adventists, practitioners of Sharia law and worshippers of the Reverend Moon in one cosy and politically correct embrace.

'So you're in favour of women being denied education and treatment in hospital, or being whipped for wearing trousers?'

'Of course I'm not,' she explained patiently, as though to a child. 'I was brought up in a different cultural tradition.'

And damned lucky for you, I thought, as I inspected her page-boy cut and scarlet nails; you might have a bit of a tough time in Kabul. 'You don't believe in a justice which transcends all cultural traditions?' I asked them both in a voice so unexpectedly resonant that several of the assembled old boys and their girlfriends turned to look at me in alarm.

'Of course you'll say that in Court, and we'll all respect you for it.' Once again Bunty sounded as though she were soothing a difficult child. 'But we don't want the Tribunal used as a platform for politicians or, worse still, political terrorists! We don't want that, do we?'

It was a question, I thought, that didn't deserve an answer, and I gave her none. Bunty put her bright fingers against her mouth and, apparently, thought profoundly.

'Ours is a government of barristers,' she told me, 'but we're always needing more.'

'Are you?' I thought I knew what was coming.

'So many tribunals, committees needing chairmen. We're facing an alarming shortage of stipendiary magistrates.'

'That doesn't alarm me,' I had to confess.

'The Lord Chancellor's always looking for someone to appoint.'

The approach had been made, and I let it dangle in the air until Archie came crashing in with, 'At your age, Rumpole, don't you want a steady job? Get your feet under some reasonably well-paid desk?'

'I don't think so. I fully expect to die with my wig on. Now I'd better get back to the mansion flat, before it's made over.'

'Great to meet you, Mr Rumpole.' Bunty was all smiles again. 'You know we have a kind of connection. I was at Saint Elfreda's. Long after your wife, of course, but we met briefly at the OE dinner.'

So Bunty had received the same kick-start in life as She Who Must Be Obeyed. That piece of news, I have to confess, didn't surprise me in the least.

'Mr Minter is here, Sir. And he's got a doctor with him.' My clerk, Henry, rang me in my room, where I was considering the possibility of lighting an outlawed cheroot and getting away with it.

'Doctor Nabi?' I asked him.

'I don't know, Sir. I'll just check.' I slid the small cigar out of its packet while listening to the ensuing silence. Then Henry said, 'That seems to be his name, Sir.'

I had scarcely lit up before my door opened. The possibility of it being Bonzo Ballard and the smoke police caused me to dispose of the evidence. As I did so, Ted Minter and his briefcase came shambling eagerly in, accompanied by a tall, thin, brown-eyed stranger with a shy smile.

'Found him at last. This is the missing Doctor.' Ted was understandably triumphant.

I waved the Doctor towards my client's chair and asked Ted, 'How did that happen?'

'I got a call from Jamil saying he was coming to my office. That was yesterday.'

'We were worried about you, Doctor,' I said. 'No one could find you.'

'I also was worried, Mr Rumpole. I was afraid all the time they would kill me.' He spoke with a pleasant, rather breathless accent, but seemed to have, I was relieved to discover, a reasonable command of English. I wouldn't have to examine him through an interpreter.

'We may not treat refugees particularly well,' I advised him. 'Our government seems anxious to get rid of them as quickly as possible. But we don't actually cull them. We save that honour for the sheep. Now tell me, Doctor, what were you so afraid of?'

'Excuse, Mr Rumpole.' The Doctor seemed obsessed with something even more important. 'I think your waste-paper basket is on fire.'

He exaggerated. There was only a slight smouldering and a certain amount of smoke. A complete burn-out was prevented by Ted fetching a glass of water from the clerks' room on the pretext of the Doctor feeling faint. This emergency having been satisfactorily dealt with, our client went on with his story.

'They wanted twelve thousand dollars to bring me to England. I scrape for eleven in Kabul. All my saving. All I can sell or borrow. So I promise one thousand dollars from a friend. A doctor in England. But when I telephone he is gone. Gone to America. I can no longer find him. So I know they will come to find me.'

'Who will come?'

'Afghan or Russian. We call them the Travel Agents, Jamil knows. He told me to move all the time. So they don't find me easily.'

'Do you always do what this fellow Jamil tells you?'

'Jamil is a good man. He helps all those coming from my country. And he knows the Travel Agents, so he can warn us

. . . Also he told me I must come to see you. You are the one chance I have of staying in your country.'

Well, I thought in all modesty, that was probably true, and I failed to remind our client, or myself, that I had never, ever appeared in front of an Appeals Tribunal before.

So I did what I do in every case, from Uxbridge Magistrates to the High Court of Justice. I went through my client's statement with him slowly, carefully, underlining every essential fact and warning him of all awkward questions. It was the usual story of a government which believes that having God on your side excuses all brutality. The Doctor had been warned, arrested, tortured and was about to be tortured again. His refusal to take part in the maiming of prisoners had led to further warnings. He went into hiding, and then, with the help of a Russian representative of the 'Travel Agents', escaped. If he were sent home, he would face further prison and more torture. When we had finished, the Doctor did something rather strange: he blew out his cheeks, lay back in his chair and said, 'I hope I can remember all that.'

'I should have thought,' I told him, 'that you'd find it all too difficult to forget.'

Then I told Ted Minter to have the Doctor medically examined for the signs of his various interrogations in police custody. We told him the date of his Appeal hearing and I asked if his friend Jamil would be there to help him.

'Oh no,' he said. 'Jamil is a shy man. He doesn't want to come out before the public at all.'

There is a cupboard at the end of the passage in the mansion flat in which Hilda stores old newspapers, sometimes for months on end, in case she should suddenly need to remember a recipe, or a new way with a cashmere scarf, or some juicy slice of gossip. I spent that evening turning over the copies of Hilda's tabloids until I found what I wanted – the one with the photograph of Afghan refugees being turned out of the chutney wagon. I took it into the sitting-room and studied it for a long time under the light, then I crept in beside the sleeping Hilda in our as yet unmadeover bedroom.

The Appeals Tribunal was held in a gaunt concrete and glass building off the Horseferry Road. I found a room with a notice 'Lawyers Only' pinned to the door. I went in and was preparing myself for the day ahead when an eager young man wearing glasses, a blue suit and dark hair brushed forward in a curious manner, so that he seemed to have a villainously low forehead, came in and called loudly, 'Hi, Rumpole. I'm your Hopo.'

I looked at him in a mild surmise. Did this eccentric imagine he was some strange tropical bird? 'I'm afraid I don't know what you're talking about.'

When he explained, I was not much wiser. 'I'm your Home Office Presentation Officer.'

'Does that mean you're on my side?'

'I'm afraid it means I'm against you.'

'So you're counsel for the prosecution?'

'Oh, I wouldn't say that,' he said modestly. 'I just present the facts to the Court in a totally fair and balanced manner.'

'Sounds fatal.'

'I must say it usually is. You chaps don't win many cases. Is this your first time?'

'In this particular jurisdiction,' I admitted, 'yes. I appear at the special request of our guest from Afghanistan.'

'He might be here for rather a short stay,' my Hopo smirked. 'Of course, I knew it was your first time because of the fancy dress. No one uses wigs and gowns down here.'

Reluctantly, I removed the ancient props of my profession.

Was this a Court of Law, I wondered, or another arm of the bureaucracy? I was a little reassured when we were called into the hearing to see a proper Judge seated behind a table on a small platform, even though the Judge in question was our one-time Head of Chambers, that Conservative-Labour politician (I could never quite remember which) Guthrie Featherstone QC MP, now Mr Justice Featherstone, whose judicial capacity was constantly frustrated by a deep-seated reluctance to make up his mind. Guthrie, wearing a three-piece suit and an unusually cheerful tie, was seated between a grey-haired woman, who looked as deeply concerned whether she was listening to me or my Hopo, and a middle-aged solicitor, who smiled at me throughout in a manner I found particularly dangerous. Such smiles from Judges often precede a particularly stiff sentence.

'Good morning, Mr Rumpole,' Guthrie greeted me politely. 'Glad to see you here at last.'

'Thank you, my Lord,' I answered him, ever courteous.

'Sir!' Guthrie said firmly.

I looked at him in amazement. Why was he calling me 'Sir'? Did he think I'd been promoted, knighted perhaps? Had I misheard the fellow?

'I beg your Lordship's pardon?'

' "Sir". You call me "Sir" here. Even though you'd call me "my Lord" in Court. I'm sure it's difficult for you, doing one of these cases for the first time.'

I looked nervously at my client the Doctor. Had he understood? If so, was it the end of my reputation in Afghanistan? He was listening attentively with one hand cupped behind his ear, and seemed to be nodding in agreement. Without further ado, I opened my case.

★

Some people tell their stories in Court compellingly, clearly and with the utmost conviction. They make their listeners feel the wrongs they have suffered, their fears, and well-founded outrage at any possible injustice that might be done to them. Such 'good witnesses' are often accomplished liars. Others stumble, hesitate, look fearfully round the Court as though seeking ways of escape and convince nobody, even though they may be, and sometimes are, telling nothing but the truth.

The Doctor, as he told his story, was in a category of his own. He was reasonable, controlled, clear and concise. He described moments of torture with a restraint that made them sound even more horrible. His English was surprisingly good and his manner to the Tribunal was respectful but not deferential. I would have had no hesitation in putting him into the 'good witness' class, except for one thing. His account sounded, to my ears, strangely impersonal, as though it had all happened to someone else, a close friend perhaps, who had suffered greatly but wasn't, somehow, exactly him.

Turning to Ted Minter behind me, to get another copy of another completed form, I saw a familiar figure among the few spectators. It was the bulky presence of my old friend and sparring partner Detective Inspector Grimble, who had been promoted out of his South London manor, where the Timson family carried on its business, to some more powerful position which was, apparently, shrouded in secrecy. All he'd told me, when I'd joined him for a farewell drink in the pub opposite his local Magistrates' Court, was that he was 'going international', which he hoped might entail trips abroad with lucrative expenses, in collaboration with Interpol. He was still young enough to go far. He was, I noticed, paying particular attention to the Doctor's evidence when it came to deal with money owed to the Travel Agents.

The Hopo had questions, many of which made considerable demands on my patience.

'Doctor Nabi, you say you were tortured after your first arrest.'

'Yes, I was.'

'You have seen the medical report on your condition?'

'I have.'

My heart sank a little. The medical evidence was not entirely helpful.

'It says the scars to your back were quite superficial and might have been caused recently. What was the date of your first arrest?'

'Two years ago.'

'Did you inflict some sort of wounds on yourself in order to impress this Tribunal?'

'No, of course not.' The Doctor was not outraged, only slightly amused at the accusation.

'Even if you were tortured, as you say, two years ago, have you any reason to suppose that you'd be tortured again if you returned to your country?'

'My Lord,' I rose in free-flowing outrage to object and was stopped by Guthrie's smiling 'You mean "Sir".'

'I mean "Sir". Isn't it obvious that if he's been tortured before, he's going to receive even worse treatment if he's sent back after trying to escape abroad? The regime hasn't changed. The country hasn't signed up to the Charter of Human Rights. That wasn't a question, it was simply a ludicrous assumption based on a wilful refusal to face the facts.'

'Mr Rumpole,' Mr Justice Featherstone was clearly gathering his wits for some sort of rebuke, 'as you see, we are sitting here without a Jury. No doubt a full Jury box at the Old Bailey might have been impressed by one of your floods of indignation. We, and I speak here for my two colleagues – ' (the bookends on either side of him nodded sagely) 'have to decide this matter without emotion strictly in the terms of Immigration Law on which I'm sure the Prosecutor – ' here he looked at the Hopo with untarnished approval, 'will give us the benefit of his knowledge and experience. Yes. You may ask the questions again.'

The Hopo accordingly did so and the good Doctor, having given the matter some thought, replied, 'No. You're right. I don't fear torture if I return. I fear death!'

As a piece of advocacy, I thought this was considerably more effective than my objection.

'Just keeping an eye on your client, Mr Rumpole. We're interested in the Travel Agents, of course. They're making their millions transporting human misery. That's about the size of it, if you want my honest opinion.'

D. I. Grimble often used this expression as though we might, from time to time, quite enjoy his dishonest one. Together with Ted Minter, we had sought refuge in a Horseferry Road pub which promised reasonable Guinness and beef sandwiches, a delicacy which I thought might, given the present government's handling of animal disease, become as rare and expensive as caviar. At the other end of the bar my Hopo, apparently satisfied with his performance, was laughing loudly with three distinctly personable young Home Office secretaries. Doctor Nabi had remained in the Tribunal building and, after swallowing a handful of vitamin pills and a glass of water, was refreshing his memory from his notes.

'Our chap has a lot to say about the Travel Agents,' I reminded Grimble. 'Russian Mafia, some of them.'

'He's in fear for his life if he can't pay them.' Ted was looking for help from a friendly officer.

'I think we may have got very close to one of the principal villains.' The Inspector sounded justifiably satisfied. 'That's why we want to keep an eye on your client, now he's emerged from the shadows, Mr Rumpole. Entirely for his own protection, of course.'

He was looking at me steadily. I had a curious feeling that the pieces of what had seemed a haphazard jigsaw had locked together, and I thought I knew what the Detective Inspector really meant.

The police observation, by WPC Mary Longcroft and DS Stewart, wearing casual clothing and driving an unmarked Ford Fiesta, was tactful but efficient. After he left the Court at five-thirty p.m., my client took a taxi to a discreet address in Devonshire Place which was known to house a massage parlour offering more exotic services to regular and affluent clients. He emerged and took another taxi to an Indian restaurant in Kensington High Street, where he ate Tandoori chicken with vegetable curry and drank mineral water and strong black tea. He walked to the Kensington Odeon, where he chose the screen presenting *Message in a Bottle* starring Kevin Costner. He left the cinema shortly after ten, visibly moved.

From the Odeon, the object of scrutiny walked down towards Earls Court Road and then, turning into Longridge Road, he stopped outside a door next to, of all things, a travel agency. He had a key to unlock the door. Seconds later, a light went on in the room over the shop. The subject was seen drawing the curtains, although chinks of light revealed that the room was still occupied.

Watch was kept by WPC Longcroft and DS Stewart for fifteen minutes, and then they heard a sudden cry, perhaps a cry for help but in a language they couldn't understand. It echoed down the empty street and then died in silence. The watchers called for assistance and, when the police car arrived, the door was broken down. The subject was found apparently alive in the upstairs room.

In the search that followed, a cupboard in the wall was found locked. When the police forced the door, they saw a sight familiar, perhaps, in the prisons and police stations of some cruelly intolerant regime. A tall man with light-brown skin and soft, pleading eyes was confined in the darkness, bound to a chair, seated in the stench of his own excrement, with his mouth shut and silenced by adhesive tape.

So the real Doctor Nabi was released from custody and later found to have marks of torture on his body which could in no way have been self-inflicted. My Appeal before the Tribunal was adjourned, pending the completion of police enquiries.

'Jamil was the Travel Agent, of course. He made a fortune transporting his fellow citizens, most of whom never got to stay here, in a succession of chutney runs. Grimble and his team were nearly on to him. He was desperately in need of a new personality.'

'So he decided to become the Doctor.' Archie Prosser, the new Boy Wonder of our Chambers, had got the point.

'Exactly.'

'But if he was the Travel Agent, didn't the Doctor know him?' Elsie Prosser, the Boy Wonder's wife, was a large, motherly woman of what used to be called a 'homely' appearance. She had a sense of humour and, apart from an inexplicable attachment to Archie, considerable common sense.

'Oh, he didn't know him as the Travel Agent, or one of them. He knew him as Jamil, the kindly refugee adviser and social worker who helped him fill in all his forms and send them off.'

'What happened to the answers?'

'Jamil got them. But he told Nabi he'd heard nothing. He was getting ready to become the noble, persecuted Doctor.'

'He never turned up before the adjudicator.' The Boy Wonder was quick to spot our case's weakest link.

'Grimble doesn't think Jamil was ready then. He'd just got the Doctor out of the council house by telling him the Travel Agents were after him and he was making him a prisoner in Longridge Road.'

'He was lucky to get leave to appeal.'

'Lucky all the way. Until the end.'

'When he deceived everyone. Including you, Rumpole,' Hilda was delighted to say.

'I had my suspicions. I looked at the picture in your paper. I couldn't see anyone who looked much like our client. And then, there was something about the way he gave his evidence . . .'

'Oh, nonsense, Rumpole!' Hilda, as ever, was determined to make the most of Rumpole's fallibility. 'You know perfectly well you were completely taken in.'

There was a silence then. The Boy Wonder took in his surroundings, cast an eye round the sitting-room, helped himself to an after-dinner mint bought by Hilda for the occasion, and said words which were music to my ears. 'You know, Hilda, you've got this flat of yours exactly how I like it.'

'There's a real feeling of home here.' The admirable Elsie Prosser backed him up.

'I can't bear the way some people do their places up nowadays,' Boy Wonder further improved the situation. 'Bubbling lights in coloured tubes and plants all over the shop.'

'See-through sock drawers,' I suggested, turning the screw.

'A chap I was at school with, works in the City,' Boy Wonder was laughing in a way I found delightful. 'He's even got a hole in his sitting-room floor, like a sort of grave, you're meant to sit in it and chat!'

'What a ridiculous idea!' I heard Hilda's voice of surrender, and heard it with relief.

'What I like about this place,' Mrs Prosser kept to the theme, 'is that every dear old article of furniture looks thoroughly loved.'

'They're all things that have seen us through our married lives, aren't they, Rumpole?'

'For better or worse. Yes.'

'You know, in some ways this place reminds me of the good old Sheridan Club.'

Down at heel? I felt like saying but resisted the temptation. Inviting the Boy Wonder and his wife to dinner had proved to be a blessing in excellent disguise.

'You know, Rumpole had some sort of an idea we needed a makeover.' I was fascinated by the devious mind now revealed by She Who Must Be Obeyed.

'Oh no, you can't! Don't do it, Rumpole.' The Prossers spoke in unison.

'Well, it was just an idea . . .' I was only too pleased to cooperate with Hilda.

'I really think,' she said firmly, 'that we should tell those decorator people they're not needed. Would you agree, Rumpole?'

'Oh yes, Hilda, I most certainly would.'

It was a moment of thankfulness, and sanity returned. I lit a small cigar and Mrs Prosser accepted one also.

'I only wonder,' Archie asked, apparently innocently, 'why this arch crook and ruthless exploiter Jamil suggested you do the Appeal. I mean, he wasn't going to get a new life if you messed it up, was he?'

'I can only suppose,' I said, 'that he had heard something about me that convinced him I could win.' And at that moment I didn't know whether to feel proud or ashamed.

'Finally, Sir, with respect to the Tribunal, may I say this. There may be people, perhaps people of power and influence, who say, or think, or might wish you to find, that if an independent state inflicts horrible cruelty on its citizens because of its sincerely held religious beliefs, or because such cruelties are part of its traditions, or are believed to be for the common good, we should close our eyes, fail to condemn it, and send its refugees who come here expecting protection back to face torture and probably death. We would submit that there are values higher than local customs or traditions, or even the demands of various religious beliefs. There is a justice which believes that persecution is persecution, cruelty is cruelty, torture is torture, murder is murder, in whatever country and for whatever motive it is carried out. With those thoughts, I leave the future of Doctor Mohammed Nabi with confidence in the hands of this Tribunal.'

It was some while later that I made this final speech in a new hearing. I had spoken to Guthrie and the bookends exactly as if they were a Jury. And it worked.

Shortly after that, the Boy Wonder left Chambers for a job in the Home Office. I had a spell of gout and extreme pain. I called on the real Doctor Nabi at his practice in the Clerkenwell Road and the stuff he gave me worked extremely well.

Rumpole and the Camberwell Carrot

'Absolutely right! I quite agree. That's the only way to treat them.'

It was breakfast time in the mansion flat and She Who Must Be Obeyed was pleased to find herself in complete agreement with her *Daily Beacon*.

The way to treat whom? I wondered. Husbands? Plumbers who make you wait at home all day on the off-chance that they might condescend to call? Supporters of the European common currency? I wondered which of Hilda's bêtes noires was in for it at the moment.

'First-time drug users! Dope fiends in the making. We're too tolerant, Rumpole! We're soft on cannabis.'

'You, Hilda? I didn't know you were soft on anything.'

'We need more like him.'

'Like who?'

By way of answer Hilda passed me her paper. The centre pages were dominated by the photograph of a burly, square-shouldered man with a broken nose and bushy eyebrows. He was staring at the camera in a hostile and challenging manner and the article was headed 'PUT FIRST-TIME DRUGGIES INSIDE, by Doctor Tom Gurnley MP, the voice of common sense!'

'He could have any job he wants for the asking, if he weren't so wonderfully *loyal*! He prefers to speak his mind from the back-benches.'

Dr Gurnley's views on the death penalty (strongly in favour), the European Union, erotic advertisements in the Underground, one-parent families and asylum seekers (strongly against) were trumpeted from every chat show on radio, television and most of the newspapers on a daily basis. If they weren't interviewing him or publishing his articles, they were reporting that there was a strong movement to make the Doctor leader of his Party after its forthcoming electoral defeat.

'The thing about him is he's prepared to crack down on crime from the outset. He understands the nature of evil, which I sometimes think is more than you do, Rumpole.'

'You may be right.' Is evil a word used too frequently to explain the apparently inexplicable? Does it exist, not only in the dock but along the corridors of power, among the law-givers as well as the cracked-down-on? I could have discussed King Lear's pertinent question: 'Handy Dandy. Which is justice, which the thief?' but breakfast wasn't the right time for such debates, nor would Hilda have enjoyed a closer exploration of this subject.

'And he's such a handsome chap, isn't he, Rumpole? I mean, he looks a real *man*. Not like some of the variety we see around the House of Commons nowadays. He's got the look of a gladiator about him. Someone with a cause to fight for! Don't you agree, Rumpole?'

'I suppose so.' As I say, I wasn't in a gladiatorial mood that morning. 'Although quite honestly I couldn't fancy him myself.'

'Do try to be serious, Rumpole. I don't think you'd catch Tom Gurnley not being serious.'

'No, I don't think you would.' I had to agree with her at last.

'Oh, what can ail thee, Erskine-Brown,' I asked Claude, not for the first time, 'alone and palely loitering?'

The look he gave me was decidedly stricken. He had the appearance of a man who's just prosecuted a plea of guilty and lost the case.

'Would you like to come to the first night of the *Ring* cycle with me, Rumpole? It's only five hours with intervals.'

'Would that be Wagner?'

'Of course.'

'I'd do a lot for you, Claude. I'd buy you a drink' (we had both resorted, after the day's work done, to Pommeroy's Wine Bar). 'I see you're drinking the wine of the country. I'll take your children to the panto. I'd even get bail for you if you're thinking of committing a criminal offence. But I have to draw the line at five hours of Wagner.'

'I knew that when I asked. I knew you wouldn't come with me. Not even for the sake of our old friendship.'

'Not even for the sake of our old friendship,' I agreed. 'Not even for that.' And then I looked at the poor fish with real concern. His condition seemed unsatisfactory, verging on the dangerous. Even the Château Fleet Street wasn't having its usual calming effect. 'Do tell me, what are you suffering from, Claude?'

'A trial separation.'

'You mean an order for separate trials?' I was at a loss.

'It's not a case in Court, you idiot! It's life. Real life! Phillida and I are having a trial separation.'

'She's left you?' It was surprising but not incomprehensible. Life with Claude might become something like a constantly repeated *Ring* cycle. No doubt the Portia of our Chambers, now elevated to a High Court Judgeship, would welcome an interval.

'What've you done, Claude?' I looked at the chap, recognizing human frailty, and, in particular, the frailty of Erskine-Brown. 'Was it the au pair or Hoskins' new pupil?' I doubted if Claude would have had the enterprise to stray further afield.

'It's not me, Rumpole.' Claude seemed stung enough to put a certain amount of energy in his denial. 'I've been a perfect husband for . . . oh well, for a considerable length of time. It's Philly. She's taken it into her head we should live apart, at least for a trial period.'

'So you've got to look after the twins, cook them burgers, et cetera?'

'Oh no, Philly's at home. She's made me move out.' Well of course, a High Court Judge, like my own Hilda, I thought, is someone who has to be obeyed.

'She's made me stay at the Sheridan Club.' Claude's voice rose in misery.

My heart went out to him. I searched for consolation. 'Well at least they have girls in there now.'

'I'm not interested in girls, Rumpole,' Claude lied. 'Anyway they're all Heads of Colleges and Governors of the BBC, those girls at the Sheridan. They're as old as my aunts and I can't keep up with their conversation. Quite honestly, I just miss Philly terribly. What can I do, Rumpole?'

'Wait and see, old chap. Time cures everything. She'll be back. I'm sure she's getting lonely.'

'She's not, Rumpole! Trevor Lowe from number five Equity Court went to a birthday dinner at the Ivy and there she was, at a table in the middle surrounded by what he called her 'groupies'. They were all laughing and having a thoroughly good time.'

'Inside her,' I tried to cheer him up, 'perhaps the heart was breaking.'

'I don't think so, Rumpole. I hardly think so. Oh, what can I *do*?' If ever I heard a cry for help, Claude bleated one now, causing assorted barristers in Pommeroy's to turn and stare at him as though he were a nasty accident.

'Claude,' I said, 'after a lifetime's knocking around some frequently unsympathetic Courts I've learnt a little of the art of persuasion. Would you like me to have a word with her?'

He looked at me then, his eyes bright with gratitude. 'Oh, Rumpole,' he blurted, 'would you?'

'Rumpole! This *is* a surprise. I hope you haven't come to ask me to give some axe murderer community service.'

'I have come,' I said, ignoring the slur on my reputation, 'to ask you for an even greater act of clemency.'

My clerk, Henry, had had words with Mrs Justice Erskine-Brown's clerk on the telephone. This led me into a discreet entrance of the Great Château de Justice, the Victorian Gothic Law Courts in the Strand, where I was escorted down passages and up stairs to Phillida's room. 'The Judge is just finishing in Court,' I was told. 'She'll be here directly.' But it was nearly half an hour before she appeared, liberated as a young girl released from school, pulled off her wig, flung it on the desk, struggled out of her black, civil case gown and, crossing to the mirror, started to assess her face critically. My line about an act of clemency was carefully ignored.

'I don't look too bad, do I? For someone in sight of fifty.'

She looked, I thought, almost better than when she had

appeared, all those years ago, a nervous pupil about to brighten up Equity Court.

'You look,' I said, 'of course, the most desirable member of the judiciary. Perhaps that's why he's missing you so much.'

'Oh yes?' She flicked at her hair with a finger, and sounded unconvinced.

'I am here,' I told her, 'on behalf of Claude Erskine-Brown QC. A man of good character with no previous convictions.'

'No convictions?' Phillida gave her reflection a small, mocking smile. 'It wasn't for want of trying.'

'I understand that, in recent years anyway, his conduct has been beyond reproach.'

'Perhaps that's what's wrong with him.' Her voice seemed to indicate that, for the present at least, clemency was off the menu. 'There's not much fun to be had from someone who is beyond reproach.' From this I gathered that, faithful or unfaithful, Claude was on a loser.

'He's missing you terribly. The chap is merely a shadow of his former self.'

'He could do with losing weight.' The Judge was merciless. 'Anyway, I've met someone.'

What did that mean? I'd met a lot of people, from safe-blowers to Lords of Appeal in Ordinary. So, in his quiet way, had Claude. 'I suppose you mean you've met someone special.'

'You wouldn't approve of him, Rumpole.'

'Wouldn't I?'

'You wouldn't approve of his politics.'

She moved away from the mirror and at last, in a more friendly mood now we had got on to discussing her special person, poured me a glass of sherry from the judicial decanter.

'Some young white wig who belongs to the Workers Revolutionary Party?'

'Hardly! This one's more than a little to the right of Genghis Khan. Capital punishment, corporal punishment, Britain's for the British – you name it, he's all for it.'

'Sounds ghastly to me.'

'It isn't really. Underneath all that he's just a simple, rather innocent boy at heart. Anyway,' she sat in one of her leathery, masculine armchairs and nursed her sherry, 'you know there's something rather exciting about someone you disagree with. Claude and I never really argued with each other. I fell in love with my present chap during a quarrel about whether or not President George W. Bush is a total dickhead.'

Would I ever have dreamt, when I did my first case before some terrifying old monster at London Sessions, that I would ever sit discussing the erotic effect of an argument about the American President on a High Court Judge?

'Does your present chap enjoy the opera?' I wondered.

'Not in the least. He thought *Rheingold* was some sort of South African currency.'

'Do I know him? He's not a member of the Criminal Bar?'

'Not at all.'

'Or of the Commercial? Tax? Family Division?' I asked, although I thought the last was improbable.

'None of that. He's a Member of Parliament.'

'Anyone I've heard of?'

'Probably. He's called Tom Gurnley.' And then her phone rang. Before I could express my amazement she was smiling, one hand on her hip, chirping happily into the instrument. 'Wonderful, darling. The Ivy at eight? No worries. I've got a babysitter. Yes . . . Love you too!'

She put a hand over the mouthpiece and, in a penetrating whisper, said, 'Good to see you, Rumpole. So glad you're going out with Claude. Try and keep him out of trouble, won't you?' and then she turned away from me, back to the voice of her improbable lover. 'See you there then, our usual table.' And she blew a kiss at the mouthpiece.

'It's absolutely disgusting!'

Hilda, with an outburst of disapproval so violent that she actually hurled her *Daily Beacon*, usually a much-cherished possession, to the ground, said, 'He's let us down terribly.'

'Nothing I've done then, Hilda?'

'He was a man who seemed to have convictions, Rumpole!'

'Well, most of my clients have got them.'

'Do be serious! That was the point about him. He genuinely believed in good and evil. You don't believe in things like that, do you, Rumpole?'

'Good and evil? Of course I do. I just don't believe they often get taken straight. Sometimes they come mixed. Like a sort of cocktail.'

'Cocktail? Do you think of nothing but alcohol, Rumpole? Well, this doesn't come mixed at all. This is pure evil. And to think how we all respected him!'

At which she scooped her newspaper off the floor and gave me a view of the front page, which was decorated with the face of Mrs Justice Erskine-Brown's favourite politician. 'ANTI-DRUG MP CHARGED WITH POSSESSION' screamed the headline, followed, in only slightly smaller type, by ' "Gurnley lights up a spliff" ', by our reporter on the spot, Angela Illsley.'

I hoped my face, as I read the story, expressed serious concern at the fact that Hilda's idol had, apparently, feet of cannabis resin. I'm afraid that all I could feel, at that particular moment, was quiet amusement.

★

'Serves him jolly well right,' said merciless Mizz Liz Probert. 'Cracking down on cannabis! The law's ridiculous. What does that ghastly, right-wing, out-of-date old dinosaur think he's talking about? Just make it legal. That would solve all our problems.'

'Solve his problem too, apparently.'

'Why can't we be like Amsterdam?'

I tried to think of an answer to this question. Because we didn't have little canals all over the place, and very few Dutch people. I gave up and asked, 'So you don't disapprove of cannabis smokers?'

'Get a life, Rumpole. Everyone does it.'

'Not *everyone*. I have yet to see She Who Must Be Obeyed with an enormous spliff, or Mr Injustice Graves giggling helplessly. I mean, do you think it's really good for you?'

'You should talk!' Mizz Probert began dismissively.

'Well, yes. I usually do.'

'You should talk about doing things that are bad for you. When you're wrecking your liver with Pommeroy's plonk and your lungs with small cigars.'

'Let's get this entirely clear! You're against a law stopping people smoking dope, but all for a law stopping me smoking small cigars?' This was a twist in the ethics of political correctness which surprised even me.

'We didn't actually make a law, Rumpole. We didn't put it through Parliament.'

'But you enforced it all the same.' I breathed in the disappointingly fresh air of my room in Chambers. 'You and the other members of the smoke police. Soapy Sam Ballard and Claude Erskine-Brown.'

'Claude Erskine-Brown.' Liz Probert's manner changed. No longer the confident legislator of modern times, the girl whose life had already been securely got, she sounded uncertain and vaguely troubled. 'I'm worried about him.'

'The fellow,' I explained as best I could, 'is going through a bad patch.'

'He hangs round me,' Liz complained. 'He comes into my room and sits down. Then he talks for a long time about nothing very much. Is something wrong with his home life?'

'Practically everything. He's moved into a dusty old gentlemen's club in Whitehall which has now admitted Claude and an assortment of clubbable ladies. He's suffering Phillida deprivation.'

'Where's she gone?'

'Nowhere. They're having a trial separation. It's a terrible trial for Claude, so anything you can do . . .'

'He asked me to go to the opera with him.'

'He asked me too.'

'You didn't go?'

'Pressure of work.' I now felt guilty and hoped that Mizz Liz would show the poor fish more generosity. 'You'll enjoy that.'

'Will I? Apparently it's one called *Twilight of the Gods*. It's not one of the long ones, is it?'

'I believe it does take a certain amount of time for the sun to set.'

'I just hope Claude doesn't start getting ideas. That's all.'

'Having seen Claude conduct his cases over the years, I can assure you that he hardly ever gets ideas.' I did my best to encourage her.

'He needs help, Rumpole. That's what I've always admired about you. Your heart goes out to people who need help.'

'My heart's finding it a little difficult to go out to Doctor Gurnley.'

'It's gone out to some pretty doubtful characters in the past.'

'Perhaps.' I had to recognize the force of Mrs Justice Erskine-Brown's argument. 'But not to anyone who wanted to abolish Juries or reintroduce death by judicial strangulation.'

'The Judge wants to see you again as a matter of urgency, Mr Rumpole. She seems a bit keen on your company, Sir,' was what my clerk had said when he brought me the message. So I'd crossed the road again and threaded my way to Phillida's room in the Palais de Justice. She was out of her wig and gown now, a distraught woman asking me to do her an unlikely favour.

'You're a taxicab, Rumpole! You're committed to giving a ride to anyone who hails you. You don't have to *like* them, Rumpole. You know as well as I do you can probably do their cases better if you *don't* like them particularly. Then you can see all the dangerous points against them. For God's sake, we've known each other for so long, have you ever turned down a client because you didn't agree with his politics?'

'Well, no . . . But . . .'

'Don't give me "buts", Rumpole. I remember that was one of the first things you said to me when I was a pupil. "You're an old taxicab, Miss Trant," you said. I took it as something of an affront to my personal appearance.'

There was a pause and she looked at me. She was no longer the daring Judge who had flicked a lock of hair as she looked at herself in the mirror. Now the moment of the youthful pupil she spoke of seemed to be vanishing further into the past.

'Look, Rumpole. I know you don't like anything about Dr Gurnley . . .'

'It's odd how retaining the title "Doctor" is a mark of some unlovable people. When you come to think of Dr Goebbels, Dr Fu Manchu, Dr Crippen, Dr Death . . .' I could have gone further but decided to comfort her distressed ladyship. 'He must make lots of money from all these articles. It'll be a headline case. He can brief an expensive silk.' Why didn't the spliff-smoking hard-liner employ a Queen's Counsel? 'I suppose if I really wanted to do him down I could offer him Soapy Sam Ballard QC, the so-called Head of our Chambers.'

'I've told Tom. The worst thing he could do is choose some high-profiled, high-priced and famous silk. He'll look as though he's buying his way out of trouble.'

'And he won't look like that if he hires me?'

'Well hardly, Rumpole.' She gave me a faint smile.

'So he wants justice on the cheap?' I was, I have to confess, a little riled, a touch put out at the suggestion that I was, to put it as kindly as possible, the bargain basement of the legal profession.

'It's not that either, Rumpole. He wants to win.'

'And he thinks I can do that for him?'

'I told him that if I were ever in trouble, I'd rather have you appearing for me than the most famous silk in the business.'

This was flattery, pure and unadulterated. Naturally I lapped it up.

'You honestly told him that?'

'Cross my heart.'

'And you have all that faith in me?'

'I've always had faith in you, Rumpole. As an advocate, I mean. I know little of your private life.'

'My private life? There's really not much to know.' But

then, more out of habit than anything else, I asked her, 'Has he got a defence?'

'Why don't you see him and find out?'

'You mean put my toe in the water?'

'Before taking the plunge.'

'Just tell him one thing. Tell him to go for Trial by Jury.'

'You think he needs a Jury?'

'Yes. Explain to him, Juries are the things he wants to abolish. But now he needs one.'

As I left, something happened which I had never expected in all my years at the Bar. I was kissed firmly on the cheek by a High Court Judge.

'It was a trap, Mr Rumpole! A ruthless, deceptive, bloody-minded trap by a gutter journalist. That's exactly what it was. And I want the Court to know.'

'So you were caught in a trap?'

'A trap was set for me.'

'And you walked into it?'

'What do you mean?' Dr Gurnley looked suddenly wary.

'I mean you walked into this trap, and lit up a large, fat Camberwell Carrot.'

'I never lit up anything of the sort!' And then he seemed to feel there was something missing from his answer. 'What do you mean by a Camberwell Carrot, Mr Rumpole? Are we here discussing vegetables?'

'I realize this is your first visit to the Criminal Courts, Doctor,' I told him. 'But if you'd been round them for as long as I have, you'd know that a Camberwell Carrot is an extremely fat spliff, a king-sized cannabis cigarette, as costly as a large Havana cigar. I don't know whether they have particularly large carrots in Camberwell, but that's what it's called.'

'Look here, Mr Rumpole.' The Doctor spoke as if he were using the name of whoever was interviewing him on the *Today* programme and he had started some particularly irrelevant, evasive non-answer with a desperately friendly, 'Look here, Jim . . .' Anyway, it was 'Look here, Mr Rumpole' this time and 'I have devoted my life to speaking my mind. Particularly about drugs. If a young person smokes a "bit of pot", that leads on to a life of evil. A life of crime, madness, hard drugs, juvenile delinquency, mugging in the streets, probably –' He seemed to be searching for the ultimate depravity, 'same-sex intercourse, disease and death. The way is open to everything that's illegal and immoral, and a million small businessmen have to support it through their taxes because it creates an intolerable burden on the National Health Service. So that's why, and I'll say this in print and in Parliament, we have to have prison for the first offence. We must have a real deterrent because that's the first step on the slippery slope . . .'

'There's nothing wrong,' I interrupted him like an interviewer who sees the time's running out, 'with a bit of hypocrisy.'

'What do you mean, hypocrisy?'

'The world's full of Christians who fail to give all their worldly goods to the poor,' I told him, 'Communists who deal on the stock exchange, Catholic priests who surrender to their housekeepers, and vegetarians who fall to the temptations of a rasher of bacon. It doesn't make their beliefs any less valid. It just means that humanity is weak.'

'I don't know what you're talking about.' The Doctor looked deeply insulted.

'I'm just saying it's understandable. Very few people practise exactly what they preach.'

'How many times have I got to tell you? I have always called for prison for a first offence of cannabis possession.' Like a very old gramophone record, my conference with Dr Gurnley seemed to have got stuck in a groove.

I had been sneaking recently, I felt, round the corridors of power. I'd gone up the back stairs of the Royal Courts of Justice to the private room of a distressed Judge. Now I and Bonny Bernard, whom I had appointed solicitor in the case, had penetrated through some sort of tropical forest planted under glass in the MP's new and luxurious accommodation. There Tom Gurnley had waved us to a seat and treated us, for the first ten minutes, to the story of his life. Born the fourth son of a South London plumber, he had made his way up in the world by way of boxing and evening classes. He was, he told us, in favour of boxing being made part of the national curriculum.

'I had my nose broken before I was twenty. Every man should.'

We heard of his climb through an accountants' office to a successful business career, his chairmanship of the Croydon Wanderers football club and his emergence as a public figure.

'I say what I mean, Mr Rumpole. I think people appreciate that. They don't get that feeling with the present leadership, to whom I am, by the way, completely loyal, never mind what the papers say.'

At last we got through the life story to the night in question. He gave a party at his house in Smith Square to celebrate a win by the Wanderers. Some star players were present, together with their model girlfriends, and members of the Shadow Cabinet, who were only too pleased to have their photographs taken with a striker who looked like an old-time pirate, ear-ringed and shaven headed, and his girlfriend, the entire back of whose dress had unexpectedly gone missing. Despite the glamour of the guests, the party seemed to have been about as eventful, and with less of an undercurrent of seething passion, than our Christmas office do in Equity Court. There was no evidence of any illicit substances making their appearance until all but one of the guests had left.

She was a girl who had come, she said, with one of the Wanderers and his girlfriend. She had been in the loo at the time of the general exodus and, whether by accident or design, found herself alone with Tom Gurnley. She turned out to be Angela Illsley, principal prosecution witness and star reporter of the *Daily Beacon*.

'She wasn't there long. She thanked me for the party and gave me a kiss.'

'She kissed you?' I wondered what Mrs Justice Erskine-Brown would have said to that. 'How long did she stay?'

'Only about ten minutes, quarter of an hour.'

And when I asked him if he had happened to light up a Camberwell Carrot during that period, he gave me, once again, his speech on the misuse of drugs.

When our meeting reached this less than satisfactory conclusion, there was one further question I had to ask.

'Dr Gurnley, what are you a Doctor of ? Heart transplants? Hip replacements?'

'I am a Doctor of Communication and Verbal Persuasion at the Rogers University of Manitoba,' he announced with pride.

'Really. Did you enjoy Manitoba?'

'I never went there. I took the course entirely by post.'

I should have known better – ask a silly question and you get a silly answer.

★

Time passed. Mizz Liz Probert allowed herself to be taken to the opera. She said it lasted a long time and she slept through most of it. Every time she woke up, the Gods were still at it and Claude was holding her hand. She released herself gently and went back to sleep.

The days lengthened and I walked down Fleet Street to the Bailey in bright sunshine. We sweated in Court and the wigs scratched our thinning skulls. The daffodils in the Temple gardens gave way to roses, and a date was fixed at London Sessions for the trial of a popular MP on a charge of possession of a class-B drug. He had taken my advice and opted for a Jury.

Neither the sunshine nor the flowers had done much to cheer up Claude Erskine-Brown. The under-employed QC still loitered palely about Chambers in search of someone to talk to, or take out to dinner, or at least for a drink at Pommeroy's, so that checking back into the Sheridan Club might be delayed as long as possible. There was, however, something more determined about the man. He had, it seemed, come to some decision, fuelled, I was to discover, by equal parts of optimism and despair.

'I've made up my mind, Rumpole. I'm going for a divorce.'

Claude was sitting in my client's chair. Indeed, there seemed to be very few hours of the day when he wasn't sitting in my client's chair, hungry for company and consolation.

'Isn't that a bit desperate? I mean, it was only a trial separation.'

'Philly's had her chance.' Claude was doing his best to look ruthless. 'It's about time I got a life.'

I remembered where I'd heard that expression before, and a terrible suspicion entered my mind.

'The trouble is that Philly and I are about the same age,

and, you must see this Rumpole, it's difficult for a man to be married to a Judge.'

I tried to listen to him sympathetically, and I didn't tell him that it was a position I'd got used to over the years.

'I had the feeling that she was judging me all the time. Well, no one likes being judged, do they, Rumpole?'

'None of my clients are very keen on it.'

'So I'm thinking of marriage to someone younger. Someone more at the start of her career.'

'Have you asked her yet?'

'Asked who?'

'Liz Probert.'

'I don't know why you should think it's Liz I have in mind.' Claude looked flattered, however, as though I had recognized that he had a reasonable chance of Mizz Probert. 'I haven't asked her yet. Naturally I'm not free to do so. But she has given me a certain amount of encouragement.'

'You mean she let you take her to the *Twilight of the Gods*?'

'She leapt at the idea of coming to Covent Garden with me. Wagner, a half-bottle and sandwiches in the Floral Hall. She loved every minute of it! That's the sort of life I can offer her, Rumpole.'

'And you think she'll leap at that?'

'What girl wouldn't?'

'Oh, I suppose – hardly any.' I didn't disillusion the poor old QC, who felt happiness was within his grasp. And then his voice became more resolute and he frowned in a way he might have thought was merciless.

'I have a strong suspicion,' he said, 'that Phillida's seeing someone else. I mean why else would she want a separation?'

'I can't imagine.'

'I'm not hanging around for her agreement to a divorce,

Rumpole. I've instructed my solicitor and I'm going to have her watched. She won't get away with this. I'm keeping her under close observation.'

'You weren't invited to Dr Gurnley's party?'

'Not actually invited. No. I told you. My friend, Anthea, happens to be the girlfriend of Keith Fawcett who plays for the Wanderers. They took me with them.'

'Did you ask Anthea to do that?'

'I asked her. Yes.'

'Simply because you wanted to go to a party?'

'I was in a party mood. Yes.'

'It wasn't just that, was it?'

There was a moment's pause. Angela Illsley, 'our reporter on the *Beacon*', stood in the witness box at London Sessions and looked towards the prosecution counsel as though for advice. She was, I thought, in her early thirties, her naturally pretty face marred, at that moment, by a frown of irritation. Her evidence in chief had been clear, precise and given with every sign of conviction. But she didn't like to be contradicted.

'Why else would I want to go?'

'Let me tell you. You were a fairly junior reporter at the *Beacon*, weren't you?'

'I do my job well, Mr Rumpole, and I'm proud of it.'

'Did you want to do your job even better and see if you could get a story about a well-known politician?'

'I'm always on the look out for stories, Mr Rumpole.'

'So you didn't just go because you were in a party mood. You went there in search of a story.'

'If you put it that way, yes.'

Seldom have I played to a larger audience. The press benches were stuffed and seasoned Court reporters were squashed in with the public. Lawyers waiting for their cases to come on had dropped in to catch the highlights of our trial. Seated in the dock, wearing a dark suit and a Croydon Wanderers tie, my client indulged in rather too much smiling at the Jury. They looked a reasonable lot, a selection of variously coloured faces. There was a large, motherly black woman whom I had seen reading the *Guardian*, two young women who might have been schoolteachers, and a scholarly looking young Indian who took copious notes. They were men and women, I thought, who lived in a world more real than that inhabited by the Honourable Member.

'The sort of story you were after wouldn't be one about what a thoroughly decent, kindly and upright citizen Dr Gurnley was and how the canapés were delicious.'

'How the what were delicious, Mr Rumpole?' His Honour Stephen Millichip was a soft-voiced, gentle Judge who seemed to be constantly surprised by the rough and often brutal world to which his modest practice in the law of landlord and tenant had brought him. 'Did you say the cannabis?' He named the drug as though the word might itself cause some sort of dangerous intoxication in Court.

'No, Your Honour. Cana*pés*. We'll get to the cannabis later.'

There was a little breeze of laughter from the Jury, and Angela Illsley got briskly back to business. 'I don't think my editor would have wanted a story like that.'

'What your editor wanted was a story that proved my client to be a complete hypocrite.'

'I don't know what you mean, Mr Rumpole.'

'Do you not? After three years working on the *Daily Beacon*, are you really telling this Jury you don't know what a hypocrite is?'

It was a mistake. The black *Guardian* reader smiled broadly, but the scholarly Indian frowned with disapproval. Adrian Hoddinot, a singularly fair-minded prosecutor, who looked owlish in thick pebble glasses and always said he only kept on working to provide adequately for his Great Dane, rose with a mild rebuke.

'Your Honour, I'm sure we all enjoy Mr Rumpole's sense of humour in the robing room. I just don't think he should make jokes at the expense of the witness.'

'Yes. You mustn't think of this Court simply as a place of entertainment, Mr Rumpole.' The Judge had, perhaps, put his finger on a flaw in my character. I stood looking suitably rebuked and he went on, as though regretting some judicial severity, 'I know you'll want to rephrase the question.'

'Certainly, I'll rephrase it.' I turned back to the *Beacon* reporter. 'You wanted a story that would show my client doesn't practise what he preaches. That all his high moral talk about family life and cracking down on drugs was pure hogwash.'

'Pure what, Mr Rumpole?'

'Hogwash, Your Honour.'

I must have stopped being entertaining. The Judge wrote the word down carefully.

'When I went to the party . . .'

'When you gate-crashed the party.'

'I told you, I went with my friend Anthea.'

'Did my client know you were coming?'

'I don't know. Perhaps not . . .'

'So when you turned up uninvited, that was the story you were after.'

'I didn't know what sort of story there'd be, or if there'd be a story at all.'

There was an obvious answer to this, but now was not the moment to accuse her of invention. I embarked on the slow approach, the line of questions the witness agrees to, until, in the end, she is fixed with one she doesn't want to agree to but may be left with no reasonable alternative.

'You stayed on in the house after all the other guests had left?'

'I told you, I was in the toilet.'

'You told us that. Yes. Let's get this clear. Up to the time when you emerged from the lavatory, there'd been no sign of anyone smoking cannabis.'

'No one was doing drugs. No.'

'Had you told your friend, Anthea, you wanted to stay on after she and her friend had gone?'

'She knew I did.'

'So it was a carefully arranged plan?'

'It was a plan. Yes.'

'Where did you go, after you were the only one left?'

'I went into the sitting-room. Tom was sitting on the sofa. I think he was having a drink.'

'Did you sit beside him, and tell him it was a lovely party?'

'Yes.'

'Had you spoken to him before?'

'Not really. Not actually spoken. He'd smiled at me.'

'Did you tell him your name?'

'He didn't ask me.'

'Did you kiss him?'

'I gave him a nice kiss.' She looked at the Jury and gave them a small, confidential smile and said, 'I think he enjoyed it very much.' It was her first mistake. The motherly *Guardian* reader looked disapproving, the studious Indian mildly surprised.

'A Judas kiss, was it?'

Adrian the prosecution rose, half-apologetic. 'I think my learned friend should explain . . .'

'Certainly I'll explain. A traitor's kiss. You kissed him and made up your mind to write a story which you knew would ruin his career.'

'It's not my fault he's ruined his career.'

'Isn't it? What did you hope for when you kissed him?'

'I suppose I hoped we'd get friendly,' again she gave an unreturned smile to the Jury, 'and he'd give me a story.'

'So was the kiss enough . . . to unlock his secrets?'

'It didn't seem to be. He looked happy, as I say, but he was quiet.' A rare moment, I thought, in the life of Tom Gurnley, MP.

'And after that?'

'After that nothing much happened and I asked him if he minded me smoking.'

'Did he mind?'

'Not at all. So I got out cigarette papers and I had some . . .' She paused, and it was time to take a risk, to ask a question without knowing the answer.

'You said in your statement to the police, and in your evidence in chief, that you rolled a cigarette. That wasn't the truth, was it?'

'It was a sort of cigarette.'

'A spliff?'

She looked at the prosecutor for help, but he sighed and looked away.

'Yes.'

'Cannabis. A class-B drug?'

'Well, yes. But the police know. They gave me a warning.'

'So not being a well-known Member of Parliament means you don't have to face the inconvenience of a prosecution?'

'Mr Rumpole.' The Judge, unused to the ways of the world, asked me, in the politest possible manner, for some basic education. 'Perhaps there are some Members of the Jury who know nothing about the making of "spliffs", as you have called them. Can you help me?'

'Certainly, Your Honour. Someone has a packet of papers and rolls a cigarette packed with the dope, which may be of varying quality. It's lit and passed round among the participants, who are meant to breathe the smoke in deeply. This produces a feeling of satisfaction and giggles, although by now the end of the joint may, perhaps, be unpleasantly moist . . .'

I stopped there. Some Members of the Jury were looking at me in wild surmise. Even the well-meaning Judge had raised his eyebrows and the prosecutor said, in a penetrating whisper, 'Are you an expert witness, Rumpole?' Had I drawn too deeply on my experience of dinner with relics of the sixties during the case concerning Mrs Twineham's skeleton? To avoid further dangerous speculation, I passed quickly on to the next question.

'Did you offer him the wet end of your spliff?'

'Yes, I did.'

She had the Jury's full attention. Their disapproval was now reserved entirely for the witness.

'Was that calculated to tempt him?'

'I thought it might be fun to see how he'd react.'

'Fun? Is this whole case *fun* to you? Fun to see a public figure humiliated and perhaps destroyed?'

'All right then. I wanted to show him up.'

'And you were determined to do that, weren't you? You

had given him the Judas kiss and you were going to sell him for thirty pieces of silver.' Was I making an absurd comparison between the Honourable Member and the founder of a great religion? Undoubtedly. But the Jury, and in particular the *Guardian* reader, seemed to relish my quoting scripture in the case of the Camberwell Carrot.

'I don't know about pieces of silver . . .'

'How much did the *Beacon* pay you?'

'I got ten thousand.'

'Not bad, for a beginner. And a job?'

'I was promoted. Yes.'

'And let off your own drug offence.'

'I told you, I was warned. And I told you, he said he'd got better stuff of his own. He went to a drawer in his desk and unlocked it. He made himself this huge . . .'

'Camberwell Carrot?'

'Yes.'

'A name, Your Honour,' I hastened to bring the learned Judge up to date, 'for a particularly large marijuana cigarette.'

'Smoked in Camberwell?' The Judge was doing his best to keep up with the evidence.

'Undoubtedly,' but here I turned back to the witness, 'but never smoked in front of you in my client's house. Did he lecture you on the dangers of using drugs?'

'No.'

'How did it end?'

'Well, we chatted a bit and then he seemed sleepy. So I left.'

'Left to write a piece of rather poor fiction for ten thousand pounds. Yes? Thank you, Miss Illsley. I have no further questions.'

★

'The defence is often at its best at the end of the prosecution case. It is now. The Jury don't like Angela at all. They're perfectly prepared to disbelieve her. They don't like her kissing you, or getting away with smoking pot. They're not at all keen on traps set by newspapers. It's my belief that she sank the prosecution. As I say, they don't like her. I'm afraid they might like you even less.'

'Why shouldn't they like me?' Tom Gurnley was genuinely puzzled. 'I'm a straightforward, plain-speaking, very ordinary sort of chap.'

'If you were very ordinary they wouldn't have gone to the trouble of prosecuting you. The point of this case is to show the world that the Crown Prosecution Service can act without fear or favour.'

'I'll just go into the witness box and let them know what I think about drugs.'

'I advise against it.'

'You want to shut me up?' He looked hurt.

'In a word, yes.'

'I'm not doing it. No one's ever been able to shut me up before.' He began to shout, as though at a Party Conference.

'Perhaps they haven't really tried.'

Decent restaurants round London Sessions are few and far between, and instead of propping up some nearby saloon bar, like the other ordinary chaps, the down-to-earth MP had booked a private room in a smart hotel. So we sat before a sweeping view of the river on its way to the Thames Barrier, past Greenwich Palace to Gravesend and the sea. We toyed with lobster mayonnaise, washed down with the sort of white Burgundy unavailable in Pommeroy's Wine Bar, and discussed our tactics for the afternoon.

'Have you taken a good look at the Jury?' I asked him.

'There are two or three serious young women who might well have one-parent families. There's a powerful black matriarch who reads the *Guardian*. There's a serious-minded Indian who might remember you saying that most of London was becoming indistinguishable from the back streets of Bangladesh. I'm just afraid that you may not be a complete hit with these honest citizens.'

'I'm not afraid of them.' The MP cracked a claw as though it were the entire judicial system. 'What do you think they'll ask me?'

'How you reacted when Miss Angela Illsley kissed you. She's quite a personable young woman.'

'I returned her kiss, in a friendly way. As though I were her uncle.'

'And when she rolled up a joint?'

'I warned her about the dangers of cannabis.'

'She says you had better stuff of your own.'

'I didn't say that. I told her, I've spent a lot of my precious time fighting a war against drugs.'

'That's what you always say. All I want to know is, did you or did you not produce a Camberwell Carrot?'

As usual, the direct question seemed to silence him. I looked out at the river that had floated queens and politicians to the Tower for beheading, received desperate young prostitutes driven to suicide, and held pirates in chains waiting for the rising tide to drown them, and here I was trying to save a public figure who didn't seem able to tell me if he'd puffed at a king-sized spliff or not.

When he spoke at last he said, 'I have a friend who's a Judge.'

'Oh yes, I know you have.'

'She said you could get me off.'

'Perhaps I can. What I can't do is call you to give evidence if I know you can't deny the charge against you.'

'But you can tell them that bloody little Angela hasn't proved the case.'

'Oh yes, I can tell them that. But if you want to give evidence, you'll have to do it on your own.'

Not for the first time, I wondered why the one-time Portia of our Chambers could ever have fallen for my client's charm. It was time for me to say, 'So, thank you for the lobster.' I rose to my feet. 'I have better things to do, more serious crimes to discuss, than you and the Camberwell Carrot.'

'Rumpole.' He put a hand on my arm. He was as near, I suppose, as he ever would get to begging for help. 'My friend the Judge was right, I'm sure. I'll take your advice on this.'

So it was still on. I gave my best legal advice. 'Then keep your mouth shut,' I said. 'You can bore the House of Commons to your heart's content. Just don't start boring this Jury. I'll do my best for you.'

Whether it was the white Burgundy or the stimulating effect on the brain of a massive intake of cold fish, I was at my best with the Jury. The Judas kiss and the thirty pieces of silver figured again in my final speech. 'Is my client's whole career, his public life and his reputation, to be at the mercy of a ruthless young journalist on the make, a self-confessed drug-taker whose unreliable evidence was sold to the highest bidder? Some of you may disagree with Tom Gurnley's politics, but as a tolerant, fair-minded Jury you will still give him the benefit of the doubt in this dubious and tarnished prosecution.' And then I remembered a criminal defender who had been in his day almost as good as Rumpole, and how he had ended his final speech on behalf of a politician. 'My client,' I told them, 'got twenty-five thousand votes at the last election. But now' (and I pointed at each Member of the Jury in turn) 'he wants YOUR VOTE and YOUR VOTE and YOUR VOTE . . .' And so on until I came to the last of the twelve.

Champagne glasses were being filled in the hotel room looking out over the Thames. All had gone according to plan. Adrian the prosecutor, with his cross-examination well prepared, had looked like a golfer whose ball, teed up and ready to be sent flying towards the green, had suddenly been snapped up by a passing eagle. He was left flailing the air when the Honourable Member remained modestly out of the witness box.

The great matriarch, having emerged as foreman of the Jury, said 'Not guilty' in ringing tones whilst looking with distaste at the ambitious young reporter from the *Daily Beacon*.

'I've just about had it with this country.' My successful client, with a glass in his hand, joined me as I stood looking out across the water.

Where was the aggressive Britishness, the refusal to be part of the decadent and corrupt bureaucracy which he imagined started at Calais, the determination to keep the streets of Croydon free from the exiled snake charmers, the devious Chinese street traders, the foreign pimps he feared were marching in their millions towards the white cliffs of Dover?

'I've been thinking for a long time. It's about time I got out.'

I appeared to consider this, watching the grey river, now dimpled with rain. Then I gave my verdict. 'I think you might be wise.'

'Do you really?' He looked at me, as though in surprise.

'Well, I must say, your advice has been pretty good up to now.'

'Someone's out to get you,' I told him. 'Someone doesn't want you in line to lead your Party. Someone with friends in the Crown Prosecution Service. It's a bit of a compliment, really. Not many of the nameless multitude of dabblers in class-B drugs would be paid the compliment of a full-blown Jury trial for a few puffs of a Camberwell Carrot.'

'That's what I was thinking. They might try and cook up another case.'

Only, I couldn't help feeling, because there might be something left around to cook.

'I've been offered,' he lowered his voice so that Bonny Bernard and the waiter might not overhear the story and tell the newspapers, 'the chairmanship of a very large sports and leisurewear company in New South Wales. I know it's not the Party leadership. It may not lead to Downing Street. But the pay's good, and I might get a look at the sun occasionally.'

'Take it,' I told him without hesitation. 'If you want my advice, you'll take it.'

'Caroline!' He called loudly to his secretary as he moved briskly away from me. 'Get the Aussies on the mobile. Wake them up if necessary.'

He left me staring at the river. I thought of the hulks packed with poachers, pickpockets, stealers of watches and handkerchiefs, who chose deportation as an alternative to hanging, and who floated down the grey river as their first stage on a journey to an unknown and almost empty continent. Then Tom Gurnley returned to me, smiling.

'You know,' he said, 'from the way you described smoking a spliff to that Judge, I'm sure you've had a bit of experience of the stuff too, haven't you?' And then he winked. That did it.

'I will eat with you, drink with you, defend you in Court. But I won't wink with you,' I told him, and so I left.

'It's ridiculous, Rumpole! Just look at it. Isn't it absurd?'

Claude handed me a document, and a glance revealed that it was a private detective's report. I remembered that he had threatened to have his wife kept under close observation. I looked at the end and saw that it was signed by no less a person than 'Fig' Newton. Ferdinand Ian Gilmour Newton had dug out golden nuggets of information in many of my cases. He is, I have always maintained, the best of the somewhat unreliable band of private eyes. His ancient mackintosh, collapsing hat, lantern jaw, watchful eye and occasionally dripping nose, the product of much open-air observation in all weathers, don't make him an immediately attractive figure, but he is a bloodhound after a guilty secret. As I began to read his report, I was dreading the revelation of some amorous encounter between the Phillida I had known and loved and the Honourable Member due for deportation.

'I'm pleased to be able to report that I think we have struck gold at last,' Fig Newton began his account in a typically modest manner, 'due to skilled observation maintained in difficult conditions.'

'Have you ever met Fig Newton?' I asked Claude.

'Never set eyes on the fellow. Go on, Rumpole, read it.'

It was a different Claude that had entered my room, no longer palely loitering but purposeful, lively and suffering from a deep sense of outrage.

I commenced observation on the house in Islington at 19.00 hours. At 19.15 the young girl I know as a part-time babysitter rang at the bell and was admitted by Hedwig, the au pair, whom I knew from past enquiries to be due for her evening off. At 19.30 a radio taxicab arrived. At 19.35 Dame Phillida Erskine-Brown (hereinafter referred to as 'the Judge') emerged from the house and entered the said radio cab. I followed in the vehicle in which I had kept observation (details of petrol charges and mileage are included in the overall sum set out at the foot of this report). The taxi took the Judge to the Ivy restaurant in West Street. I was able to observe her enter the restaurant and I should at this juncture make it clear that the Judge was dressed, as I would phrase it, 'up to the nines'. She was wearing a well-cut black dress, with several pieces of jewellery. I came to the conclusion that she had come to meet 'someone special', and subsequent events confirmed this view.

I was fortunate to secure a parking spot and I approached the Ivy restaurant on foot. A man of Irish extraction wearing a top hat tried to prevent my entry but I told him I was booked in and walked past him. The young lady in charge of the coats was similarly discouraging. However, I got past the glass doors into the dining area and was met by a further young woman in a black trouser suit. I again claimed to have a booking and, as she went to check at the desk, I was able to obtain a view of the assembled diners.

I have to report that the Judge was there with another man. They were both smiling, and talking in an animated manner. Her hand was on the table and he was holding it. During the minutes for which I kept observation, the Judge made no attempt to withdraw her hand. I would describe the man in question as 'furtive', 'sly looking', 'talkative' and not, I would have thought, 'attractive to women'. He had mouse-coloured, receding hair, a weak chin and wore spectacles and a dark, pinstriped suit. Before I could approach the table more closely, the girl in the black trouser suit, by now accompanied by a small Maître d' with a determined look and a trace of a cockney accent, told me in no uncertain terms that I had no booking for that night or indeed any other night, and he invited me to leave immediately. As I left the Ivy restaurant, the man in the top hat suggested he call me a cab. I declined, having my own transport and not wishing to put the client to further expense.

At 22.00 hours the Judge left the Ivy restaurant with the 'furtive-looking' man I have previously described. He seemed to be looking about him in some fear of observation, but he didn't notice me in my vehicle parked up in the shadows of West Street. The parties got into another cab. I noticed that the Judge gave money to the man in the top hat, her date of the evening having clearly protested that he had 'no change'.

At 22.15 the parties stopped outside a large building, in clear need of a lick of paint, in one of the streets behind Whitehall. I was able to follow them into the hallway, where the 'furtive man' asked a sleepy porter for 'The key to my bedroom.' They both then took a lift to an upper floor. I was unable to follow as the sleepy porter asked me my business, and when I said, 'Just looking around. What is this place?', he said, 'The Sheridan Club. Members Only' and instructed me, again in no uncertain terms, to leave. Seated in my vehicle, I kept observation on the entrance of the Sheridan Club until 03.00 hours on the nineteenth. Neither the Judge nor the 'furtive' companion had emerged by that time, from which I deduced that intimacy had undoubtedly taken place.

'"Furtive! Sly looking! Weak-chinned! Not attractive to women." Would you describe me like that, Rumpole?'

'Not in a million years.' I resisted the temptation to say 'yes'.

'So how could this ridiculous Fig person get me so wrong? Hasn't he got eyes in his head?'

'You can't mean –' a wonderful prospect opened before

me, 'that it was you having dinner with Phillida in the Ivy?'

'Of course it was. She rang me up last week. Out of the blue. She said something had happened to change her mind. So we made a date for dinner. It went amazingly well. Quite like old times. In fact . . .'

'Of course, the Sheridan Club! I ought to have realized.'

'This Fig Newton, Rumpole – what am I going to do? He wants me to pay him two hundred pounds for telling me that I had dinner and slept with my wife!'

'Take my advice,' I told him. 'Count it cheap at the price.'

'Oh, all right.' Claude looked temporarily depressed at the prospect, but soon cheered up. 'I want to thank you, Rumpole, for all you've done to bring me and Philly together again. I brought you a small gift.'

He walked away with an unusual spring in his step; a man, I thought, who had recovered, at last, a little of the snap in his celery. He had left me a packet of my favourite small cigars. I lit one, and blew a perfect smoke-ring at the ceiling of my room.

Rumpole and the Actor Laddie

'Mr Rumpole! Your timing! My dear, it's something to die for. And the hand gestures! So telling. That wonderful sniff of contempt, just the way Larry used to do in *The Merchant*. Of course, I've only had the opportunity of seeing your perf from the gods at the Old Bailey. And I don't believe you saw the last thing I did. My Adam the gardener in *As You* with the Clitheroe Mummers. A small part, of course, but I think I made a little jewel of it. That was in '84, or was it '85? It's difficult to get cast when you're not young, and definitely not prepared to take your clothes off. That's why I'm thrilled that we're working together at last. I've dreamed and dreamed, I promise you, my dear, of playing opposite the great Rumpole of the Bailey!'

Was my timing so good? Quite honestly, I had never thought about it. And yet I was half-pleased to get a tribute from the client who had told me at the outset that he was 'in the business', and when I asked what business that might be, he had given a light laugh and said, 'A poor player, an honour I share with Garrick and Irving and the late great Sir Donald Wolfit. My crown is a little tarnished now, but some old theatre-goers won't easily forget my Benvolio, my French Ambassador – above all my Rosencrantz in the Danish play. I have, it's true, been resting for, well to be honest with you, getting on for quite a while, which is why I'm so looking forward to our forthcoming engagement. I know I haven't lost the trick of holding an audience. I just hope I won't have trouble remembering the lines. I fear I'm no longer the "quick study" I was.'

The elderly man talking with the volubility of someone emerging from years of silence had a pink face, a monkish fringe of grey hair and the appearance of an elderly cherub run to fat. He wore a light-grey suit, strained at the buttons, suede shoes and a bright-pink tie. A voluminous silk handkerchief billowed from his breast pocket and he smelt of some pungently seductive eau de toilette. His name, inscribed on my brief, was Percival Delabere, and the venue in which we were to perform together was, I am sorry to say, the London Sessions, where Percival was engaged to play the lead in a fairly ordinary charge of theft.

When he was no longer, as he would say, 'in demand' as an actor, Percy Delabere ('Call me Percy, dear boy. Johnny G. and Dame Edith always did') eked out his living on a small income left to him by an aunt and occasional speech lessons to puzzled West Indians or Spanish waiters who wanted to talk in the singsong tones of long-dead actor-managers. He was able to afford a bedsitting room on the top floor of a crumbling Victorian house in Talbot Square, near Paddington Station. This undesirable residence was the property of a Miss Hunter, a large, untidy woman, a solitary gin drinker whose quarters and financial affairs were in a perpetual muddle. She fussed over her younger, more attractive tenants and took only a perfunctory interest in the fading career of the old actor on the top floor.

The circumstances which led to our meeting, and his complimentary remarks about my perf, in the conference room at the London Sessions were unfortunate. During his long rests it was Percy's practice to wander about the house, going into other people's rooms in order to bore them with reminiscences of Larry, John G. and the great Sir Donald Wolfit. On the afternoon in question, Miss Hunter had pottered round to the off-licence and left her door open. It was agreed that Percy had popped into her room to pay his rent and, apparently for want of anything better to do, had examined some items of the landlady's jewellery which she had left in a jumble of possessions on a marble-topped table under a tarnished mirror. A Mr Crookshank, a retired insurance salesman, had passed Miss Hunter's open door and seen Percy slip her most valued possession, a diamond and emerald ring, on to one podgy finger and stand admiring the effect of it in the looking glass. Later Miss Hunter announced that the ring was missing, and Percy made a considerable investment in new pink shirts, a silk dressing-gown and a purple, spotted bow tie from a posh shop in Jermyn Street.

'How did you afford all that?' I asked Percival.

'Poor as I am, Mr Rumpole, I had made savings. And one must keep up appearances. That is very important. You never get offered anything if you don't keep up appearances.'

I thought that producers would hardly be hurrying to Percival's door at the hot news that he had bought a new dressing-gown, but I didn't say so. Instead I came to the very heart, the nub of the matter. 'I suppose you'd better tell me now. Did you take the landlady's ring?'

'Mr Rumpole.' There followed a long pause, which, although no doubt meant to be dramatic, soon became tedious. And then, 'Do you really have such a low view of my profession?'

Ignoring the fact that he seemed to find no appreciable difference between the Bar and the stage, I did my best to focus the man's attention. 'That's a question you'll have to answer "Yes" or "No" to soon.'

'Not now, Mr Rumpole.' He held up a warning hand. 'I shall tell the full story when I enter the witness box.'

'You'd better not enter it until I know what you're going to say.'

'My dear! Would you deny me the witness box? Am I to be a mere extra, a super, a spear-carrier with no lines? My crown may be a little tarnished now, but I think you can rely on me to play the lead. I promise I shall not disappoint.'

'You'll go into the witness box over my dead body,' was what I should have said, but I weakly agreed to call him. How could I deny the old actor laddie the only leading role he was likely to get?

I did say, 'I assume you'd deny keeping the ring?'

'Mr Rumpole. It's for you to make assumptions. It's for me to play the lead. To the best of my poor ability.' And that, of course, is exactly what he did.

'Mr Rumpole, can't you control your client?'

'I'm afraid, Your Honour, that is quite impossible.'

Why had I ever allowed Percival to take centre stage? We were a quarter of an hour into his evidence, he was in full flow and his Honour Judge Archibald – 'Artful Archie' to his many detractors, owing to his many ingenious ways of persuading Juries to convict – was clearly in the throes of terminal irritation.

The trial had started quietly. Miss Hunter, voluminous and somewhat confused, told the story of the missing ring which Mr Crookshank had last seen on Percy's finger. And then Percy had gone into the witness box and taken the oath in the hushed tones of the Prince of Denmark addressing his father's ghost. After a few routine questions, he ignored me and became Mark Antony, orating to the Roman plebs.

'My friends and fellow countrymen on the Jury,' his voice was low and throbbing, 'may I take a moment of your time to speak of my humble self? I am a poor player that struts and frets his hour upon the stage – in my case this witness box – and then, perhaps to your relief, will be heard no more . . . I have lived for my art. I have done my poor best to dedicate myself to that perpetual challenge which is the theatre. I have sung with Shakespeare and argued with Shaw and, yes, I am not ashamed to confess it, on occasions lost my trousers with Ray Cooney.' Here he waited for a laugh which never came. 'Such a career teaches passion. It teaches love of the language. What it cannot teach is sensible behaviour and self-restraint . . .'

After a good deal more in the same vein, Artful Archie made his irritated interjection, so I attempted to drag the wandering thespian back to the point at issue, and I put the question to him bluntly. 'Mr Delabere, do you agree that you put Miss Hunter's ring on your own finger and surveyed the effect in the mirror?'

'Members of the Jury. You will remember the line in the Moorish play – I speak of *Othello* – about the base Indian who threw a pearl away, richer than all his tribe?'

'Mr Delabere!' I have to confess that the Rumpole patience, never my strongest asset, was wearing extremely thin. 'Let's forget the Moorish play, the Danish play, or indeed the Scottish play for a moment and concentrate on one simple fact. Did you put Miss Hunter's ring upon your finger?'

'I imagined, for a moment, that I was playing the Doge in the Venetian play. I remembered that they wore rich jewellery.'

'For the last time. Did you put on the ring or not?'

'I did.'

The relief at actually getting an answer gave me confidence to move on to the next, most dangerous question. 'And did you take it away with you, Mr Delabere? Did you steal it?'

Percy treated us to one of his famous pauses, during which I held my breath and Archie sat with his pencil poised to take a note. When Percy spoke again it was to treat us to yet another oration.

'Members of the Jury. I have taken the liberty of calling myself a poor player, and poor I am. It has been a constant worry to keep myself in those few necessities – a good suit, a few decent shirts, an attractive tie – which are vital if you wish to keep in the swim, to be seen and thought of as a character actor, now my juvenile days are over, who is constantly "available". Those who devote themselves to their art do not expect to be richly rewarded. We don't ask for yachts, Members of the Jury, or Old Master paintings, or a Rolls-Royce motor car. What we, perhaps, have the right to expect is a decent standard of living, which would leave us free to dream, to create, to study and, when in work, do our job without the haunting fear of future poverty. So what am I saying? Did I steal the ring? Yes. I stole the ring. I announce it publicly! I announce it proudly. Miss Hunter has boxes of jewellery, most of which she never wears. You have seen her – her fingers are glittering, her neck is loaded, with semi-precious trinkets. That ring, Members of the Jury, is the tribute the property owner pays to the artist. Judge me if you will. Call me guilty if you must. But don't deny me your understanding or your mercy, which, like the blessing of the Almighty, transcends all human laws!'

At which point, I promise you, Percy Delabere clung to the front of the witness box and bowed as though acknowledging the wildest applause after the most exhausting performance. The Jury sat in stolid silence and the only voice heard was that of Artful Archie, who sounded content that the old actor had convicted himself without needing any assistance from the learned Judge.

'Mr Rumpole, I imagine you will now advise your client to change his plea.'

'I see it's nearly one o'clock.' I decided to play for time. 'Perhaps I might take his instructions during the lunch-time adjournment?'

'Very well. But in view of what he has now told us, I must cancel his bail. Delabere will be taken down to the cells. Back here at two o'clock, Members of the Jury.'

Confronting the actor laddie in the cells before having a drink would have been like having an operation without an anaesthetic and I decided against it. I ordered a pint of Guinness in the pub across the road and was about to consume it with a slice of pork pie and pickle when 'Spider' Wilkinson, the counsel for the prosecution, so-called because of his thin arms and legs which seemed to stretch out in all directions and his solemn, bespectacled face, came in and greeted me with, 'Rumpole! You lucky bastard!'

'Lucky? To have a client who is so clean off his head that he makes a totally unnecessary confession to the Jury in a performance of such unutterable ham that I blushed to hear it? Do you know, that idiotic thespian complimented me on my timing! His timing was perfectly judged to get him a long rest in Wormwood Scrubs.'

'Did you think you could get him off?'

'We had a chance. There was no evidence he actually sold the ring, or even kept it.'

'He didn't.'

'What do you mean?'

'Just that dear old Miss Hunter searched through her hand-bag, apparently a lengthy undertaking, late this morning and found a receipt from a jeweller. She'd taken the ring in to be repaired long after your client tried it on. We rang the shop and it's still there. When we go back I'll have to tell Archie. He's not going to like it.'

Strangely enough, when I brought the good news to Percy, he also seemed disappointed. When I asked him why on earth he'd shopped himself to the Jury, I could make no sense of his reply.

'It seemed right somehow, Mr Rumpole. The perfect dramatic ending to what I flatter myself was a moving speech, powerfully performed. I stood before them, I thought, a heroic victim and not a foolish old actor who tried rings on for fun. I think it was my finest performance.'

I left Percy Delabere then, having resolved never, under any circumstances, to work with him again.

Rumpole and the Teenage Werewolf

'We've tried, Mr Rumpole. No one can say we haven't tried. His own telly, his own telephone number.'

'He's on line, Mr Rumpole. He can access the world from his own bedroom.'

'Trainers. And Puffa jackets. You can't imagine the amount he's cost us in trainers.'

'And we've always done our best to be fair to him. Not judgemental.'

'Chris is always so fair-minded. He tries to reason with him.'

'It's very hard, Mr Rumpole, to reason with a slammed door.'

'Chris understands young people. He gives his time freely to a youth club in Worsefield. He helps them to become computer literate.'

'It's the struggle, Mr Rumpole. Every day's a struggle. Will there be a row? Has he gone missing? It's a nightmare for his mother. She's losing weight over it.'

The couple who sat in my clients' chairs were what She Who Must Be Obeyed would have called 'thoroughly nice people'. They might qualify to represent the best of Middle England, modest and intelligent, capable of serious concern but also able to make jokes at their own expense. They were,

I thought, the type of people who supported the local Oxfam shop, gave generously to hospices, read to the blind, whipped round for funds to help the victims of floods and earthquakes in distant parts of the world and organized free trips to the seaside for the poor and elderly.

They had come with their local solicitor, an amiable old bird named Beazely who looked as if he'd be more at home shooting pheasants than fighting a prosecution for assault and offences under the Prevention of Harassment Act. Notably absent was the sixteen-year-old they had been talking about with such weary resignation. Ben was Hermione Swithin's son and her husband Christopher's stepson. He was due to make his criminal debut before Hartscombe Crown Court.

The family history was also typical of Middle England. Hermione had met Martin Cutler at University and given birth to Ben when she was twenty-three. Cutler, apparently a part-time journalist and full-time drunk, had disappeared to America with Hermione's best friend and little or nothing had been heard from him since. Hermione's first job was as Christopher Swithin's secretary and they were soon in love. 'Ben was four when Chris took him on, Mr Rumpole. He's treated him just as though he was his own son. Our Caroline's different from him in every way.'

'We call Ben the teenage werewolf,' Chris explained and they both laughed gently, apparently comforted by this description.

'Not to his face, of course. To his face we always try to build him up – give him confidence.'

'Caroline's such a sweet character.' Hermione looked gratefully at Chris, as though congratulating him on not having brought any of her first husband's destructive genes to infect the character of their daughter. 'She's always smiling.

She's only ten but you can tell she's going to grow up as a thoroughly adorable person.'

'She just wants everyone to like her, that's our Caroline.'

'The teenage werewolf doesn't care if no one likes him at all.'

'When we moved into Merrivale and Chris could do all his work from home we thought Ben'd be so happy. All of us together in one place.'

Was all the family being together in one place a perfect recipe for happiness, I wondered? Not, perhaps, for the Macbeths or the Agamemnons in their houses of doom, but Merrivale sounded, from the Swithins' account of it, a highly desirable residence. It was an old brick and flint farmhouse with magnificent barns from which the sheep and cows had long gone, and the hay moved out to make way for Christopher's computers and office equipment, installed so he could run his particular dot.com business from a part of what was left of rural England. Both the children went to state schools in Hartscombe, the nearest town, some ten miles from Merrivale ('If people like us don't support the state system it'll never get any better,' Hermione had told me). At sixteen, Ben was facing his A-levels and had been booked into Hartscombe College, where his attendance was sporadic and the lectures were occasions when he found it convenient to catch up with his sleep.

'That's par for the course with teenagers, Mr Rumpole.' Chris was at his most tolerant. 'That's what we'd been told to expect. We thought he'd grow out of it. We could see sometimes – when he bought Hermione a birthday present with his own money, for instance – a light at the end of the tunnel. We could live through all that. This is something quite different. We never thought he'd take to serious crime.'

'He says he didn't do it,' Hermione reminded her husband.

'Of course he does. And we've stood by him. That's why we've come to you, Mr Rumpole.'

The Swithins were involved with the law because of a girl called Prunella Haviland, just seventeen and also at Hartscombe College. 'Everyone says she's so attractive but Chris thinks she's nothing out of the ordinary,' Hermione told me. 'He used to pick her up on the school run, until suddenly her father decided to take her. That was when the e-mails started coming to Prunella.' It was the e-mails that constituted the harassment and supplied the evidence of guilt in the case of the teenage werewolf. In the earliest days they were amorous, then openly obscene, lecherous and full of promises to perform eccentric and sometimes dangerous acts of love. At one stage, walking through a lane in Hartscombe after dark, Prunella had felt she was being followed and some-one close behind her fastened his arms round her. It lasted only a few seconds, but she felt a kiss on the back of her neck before she struggled free and ran. After that she never walked alone through the town, by day or by night. She was not molested again, but the e-mails continued thick and fast. They clearly emerged from the computer bought, at considerable expense, to propitiate the werewolf one Christmas and installed, among other costly technology, in his bedroom at Merrivale.

'We knew he was difficult, selfish, utterly incapable of caring about how his mother or I felt. We didn't know he was a criminal. Do what you can for him, Mr Rumpole.'

'You see how it is.' Hermione gave her husband a small, sad smile. 'Chris loves Ben. He's the only son he's never had.'

And then, it seemed, the conversation dried. Neither of the concerned adults had any more to say about the accused werewolf except that he had been given the address, and the telephone number, and even a map of the Outer Temple so that he could find Equity Court and meet his defender. He'd been to a party in London the night before and had promised them he'd be at the conference in my Chambers but, by now, it was time to give him up. It had happened before and would probably happen again, and yet again. He was on bail and kept away from school for the sake of Prunella. Perhaps he'd gone home by now, perhaps they'd find him there, perhaps not. Hermione looked at me, apologetic, confused, as though she had no reasonable explanation to offer for the human being she had brought into the world.

In the silence that followed I was looking once again at the printed-out e-mails.

'It's interesting,' I said. 'They're outrageous, of course. But some of these messages are quite poetic.'

Chris Swithin was looking at me with deep disapproval. Clearly I had said the wrong thing, and soon after this the couple left.

When were teenagers invented? I tried to remember myself slightly spotty, a great deal thinner, in a cold boarding school beside an unfriendly sea, with a headmaster whose role model appeared to have been Captain Bligh of the *Bounty*. Despite all the discomforts, and the occasional terrors of the place, I had no thought of leaving it. I tolerated my parents, and my father's often-repeated stories. I understood his reluctance to spend more time than was absolutely essential with an adolescent whose favourite reading was *Notable British Trials*. I put up with my mother's resigning herself, with a sigh, to the fact that my failure to keep my room tidy would make it unlikely that I would ever marry. I kept the other boys friendly by telling them stories and provided defences for them when they were faced with serious charges of giggling in chapel or introducing white mice into the divinity class. I sent no obscene communications to girls, indeed I knew hardly any girls to send them to. On the whole, I would say I was a more conventional character, politer, more easily imposed upon and with a respect for authority which had dwindled, rather than increased, over the years.

'Were you a teenage werewolf?' I asked Mizz Liz Probert as we sat together in the Tast-Ee-Bite in Fleet Street. I was fortifying myself with a bite of breakfast before making my way down to Ludgate Circus, the Palais de Justice and my customers in the cells.

'I told my mother she was stupid,' Mizz Liz admitted. 'I did that quite a lot.'

'Are you ashamed of that?'

'Not really. It was perfectly true. Someone had to say it. My father didn't dare.'

'Then I suppose,' I told her, 'teenagers were invented around the date of your birth.'

'Not all teenagers are terrible.' Mizz Liz sprang to their defence. 'Although I must say I've got one odd one now.'

'You've got one?' She seemed too young. 'Is he, or she perhaps, giving you hell as a mother?'

'Don't be silly, Rumpole. Not my child, my client! At least I've been told I'm going to get the case. Nasty charges of harassment and assault. I got rung up by a firm of solicitors in Hartscombe.'

'Is the boy called Ben Swithin?'

'You've got it, Rumpole!'

The teenage werewolf was Mizz Liz's client? This was deeply disturbing and I sought for the only possible explanation. 'You'll be my junior?' I asked her. 'I'm going to need all the help I can get.'

'Oh, they didn't say anything about that. I got the feeling they want me to do it on my own.'

With this Mizz Liz got up, leaving me puzzled. As she left, she was immediately replaced by Soapy Sam Ballard, carrying his meagre breakfast of muesli, with hot water and lemon on the side, on a tray which he held with as much care as if he was transporting caviar and some rare wine in a cut-glass decanter. As he put down his tray and laid out his feast, he looked after Mizz Liz Probert's retreating figure.

'Nice little bottom she's got to her, our Mizz Probert. Wouldn't you say so, Rumpole?'

I was profoundly shocked at what Mizz Liz and the sisterhood of young women lawyers would have regarded as outrageously offensive. If made by our clerk, Henry, or one of the Timsons, or even my most regular client and solicitor, Bonny Bernard, it would have seemed no more than a background noise in the meaningless chatter of everyday life. None of those people would have thought of making any sort of amorous approach to Mizz Liz. Had she turned to face them, they would have been almost deferential in their approach. But this was Soapy Sam, leading light of the Lawyers as Christians, tied, you might say cocooned, by his marriage to Matey, the formidable nursing sister who manned the casualty room at the Old Bailey, ready with cough sweets or Elastoplasts and calming words for lawyers attacked by disappointed clients or the victims of bungled attempts at suicide. To hear Ballard, who had adopted self-righteousness as a way of life and regarded the lighting up of a small cheroot as a breakdown in public morality, use such an expression about any member of the Bar was like hearing a bishop break out into a couple of verses of 'The Good Ship Venus' during evensong. But now Liz was gone, and Ballard was staring at the less potentially erotic subject of his plate of muesli.

'I've been a little unsettled, Rumpole. Since you found that old photograph of the Pithead Stompers.'

'Forget it,' I advised him. 'We've all made mistakes in the past.'

'I don't regard it as a mistake, Rumpole. Perhaps . . . as a matter of regret. I can't help feeling that I enjoyed life more then.'

'You want to pick up the guitar again? Assemble the old drum kit?' I couldn't believe that Matey would welcome sessions from ageing Stompers in the Ballard home.

'Not that. Of course I'm happily married now.'

'Of course.' Why should I dispel his illusions?

'And I have my work. And the Lawyers as Christians to look after. But when I look at that photograph you so kindly gave me, I can't help remembering girls dancing the Shake. Did you ever dance the Shake, Rumpole?'

'Not within living memory.'

'Happy days. When we were young.'

'Not always.'

'No, I suppose not.'

'I've got a client now known as a teenage werewolf. Got himself involved in serious crime because of a girl. You're far safer living quietly in Belsize Park with Matey. Your days with the guitar are over. Are you going to eat that stuff, by the way?' Ballard had been toying with his muesli, putting a spoon in as tentatively as the toe of a swimmer confronted by an icy pool.

'Of course I'm going to eat it, Rumpole.' And he crunched a mouthful of what appeared to be wet, flavoured stubble. 'We all need roughage.'

I had, I felt, quite enough roughage in my life without having recourse to muesli.

As soon as I got back to Chambers, I rang the Swithins' solicitor. We had done various jobs together of an unsensational and rural nature – careless drivings, closed footpaths, stolen piglets, receiving stolen diesel – in all of which I had achieved a satisfactory level of success.

'Oh, is it you, Mr Rumpole?' The country lawyer sounded startled, as though he'd been peacefully reading *Trout and Stream* and enjoying life until he heard a voice which must have pricked his conscience.

'What do you imagine you're up to, Beazely? Have you entirely forgotten the rules of ethical behaviour which apply even to solicitors? Or was your head turned by the scrumpy or whatever it is you drink in the countryside?'

'Mr Rumpole . . .'

I could tell the man was already somewhat shaken, so I twisted the dagger in the wound. 'I have been practising at the Bar almost as long as living memory and on no occasion – you hear that? – on no other occasion has a case in which I have been briefed been offered to a junior white wig, a girl to whom the Penge Bungalow Murders may seem an historical event as distant as the Battle of Waterloo. I refer, as of course you know, to Mizz Liz Probert and the case of the teenage werewolf.'

'The point was . . .' Here Beazely attempted a stammering defence. 'The client thought . . .'

'What do you mean "The client thought"? Have you met the client? Has he spoken to you? Is he in some way related to Mizz Probert?'

'I've never met him. No. But the Swithins thought . . .'

'I know what they think. I've had an opportunity of studying the Swithins in depth.'

'They think the boy might react better to someone of his own age.'

'The boy, as you call him, has had no opportunity of reacting to me.'

'They can't persuade him to come to London for a conference.'

'Then Mahomet must come to the mountain.'

'Who did you say?'

'Don't concern yourself, Beazely, with Mahomet. A figure of speech. Just find out which evening this week it would be convenient for me to come down to Hartscombe. I can easily manage tonight. You and I will talk to the client together.'

It wasn't until the end of the week that the Swithins could take time off from their charity committees, their book-club gatherings, Chris's prison visiting and Hermione's quiz in the village hall to support the handicapped. Ben was helping out in a Hartscombe restaurant the night I visited Merrivale.

'If he wants a younger brief, I can understand that.' This was Rumpole at his most reasonable. 'But I want to hear it from the client in person. Neither of you . . .' I looked at the werewolf's mother and stepfather, comfortable but no doubt deeply concerned people, 'neither of you is in danger of youth custody.'

'He promised he'd be here by ten.' Hermione's wail was muted and polite, but it had its own brand of desperation. 'It's really too bad of Ben.'

'He sometimes stays in the restaurant talking,' Christopher told me, 'even after it's closed.'

'He talks to someone, that's encouraging,' I told them. 'If he does that there's no good reason why he shouldn't talk to me.'

'No consideration for others. No manners. Wherever young Ben came from, he didn't arrive from heaven, trailing clouds of glory.' Chris's knowledge of Wordsworth put him up a notch in my estimation.

We were waiting, this time, in Chris's study. All his computer technology was, he assured me, in the barn, and the room had an old-fashioned comfort, with a crackling log fire, armchairs, an impressive collection of books lining the walls, with the lights shining on their golden titles. We had been drinking brandy, listening to Schubert on the CD player, enjoying all the delights of a civilization which had not, apparently, rubbed off on Hermione's son. As we waited for him, conversation seemed to run out with the brandy until Chris, after prolonged and careful thought, said, 'I don't think he'll ever talk to you, Mr Rumpole.'

'We'll have to see about that.' I decided the time had come to track the werewolf to its lair. 'Oh, by the way, could I borrow your loo before I go?'

'I'm so sorry.' Hermione, who apologized for most things, was also sorry about her bathroom. 'It's up the stairs.'

'First on the left when you get to the landing.' Chris was more practical.

The bathroom, when I got to it, needed no apologies. The air had been freshened with a no doubt chemical but pleasant smell of fresh apples. The porcelain gleamed, the loo seat was of dark mahogany. The towels looked soft and inviting. Glass shelves on one side of the washbasin supported Hermione's array of lotions and unguents, her shampoos, perfumes, cottonwool buds, tweezers and electric toothbrush. The shelves on the other side were clearly Chris's, displaying his silver-backed brushes, his electric razor, Floris soap and anti-dandruff shampoo and a more masculine perfume clearly labelled 'For Men'. I suppose it was a small part of me that wanted, like the Timsons, to get something for nothing that tempted me to sprinkle a little of this on the Rumpole handkerchief. The smell was fresh, strong and reassuringly male. Smelling like that, I felt, entirely qualified me to meet and tame the werewolf.

Il Paradiso in Hartscombe marketplace was closed, but the lights still shone behind drawn blinds. After Beazely had rattled the door, it was opened by a woman in a black trouser suit. Apparently she knew my instructing solicitor as a regular customer and she was full of apologies.

'Such a shame! We've taken the last orders and the kitchen's closed. We could perhaps do you and your friend a plate of antipasti.' She sounded entirely English and had brought Tuscany to Hartscombe by way of the Sunday supplements.

'That's very kind of you,' I told her, 'but we've really come to meet one of your waiters. Ben Swithin.'

'Ben? Of course. I think he's still here. Come in, both of you.' My heart warmed to this polite hostess when she led us to a corner table and offered the apparently popular Beazely a bottle of Chianti on the house. I watched her as she went to a long table where teenage waiters, making a few pounds after school hours, were laughing together. After some persuasion she detached one of them and brought him to our table. He approached in slow motion, frowning deeply.

'Who are you?' he said. 'What do you want?'

'I want you to sit down. And have a glass of wine.'

'I don't drink. Who are you? Or what?'

'I'm a lawyer,' I had to admit, 'but don't let that put you off.'

'Mum and Dad wanted me to see a lawyer. It's like . . . I can't be bothered.'

'Why can't you be bothered?'

'Because it's useless.'

'Why is it useless?'

'Because you can't help me.'

'Suppose I told you you're innocent.' The effect was surprising. He looked at me, a long, wondering look. He was a boy, thin, narrow-shouldered, a little short for his age. His hair looked as though it had been almost shaved and was growing back to an untidy stubble. He had the eyes of his mother, large and luminous with sculptured eyelids. He sat down then, the scowl faded and he looked younger than his years and quite defenceless.

'What did you say?'

'I said you're innocent. Until they prove you guilty.'

'They won't have much trouble. Right?'

'How do you know?'

'Dad told me.'

'You call Christopher Swithin "Dad"?'

'Yes. He asked me to.'

'I see.' For a werewolf, he seemed to be singularly obliging. 'Tell me about this girl, this Prunella. She goes to your college.'

'I don't go near her. I'm not allowed. I'm not allowed to go within miles of her. Like I'm a sort of fatal disease.' All these sentences ended on a rising inflection, as though they were questions, but he required no answer. I knew about his bail conditions.

'Tell me more about Prunella.'

He picked up a table knife and, quite ineffectually, tried to saw at the edge of the table. This occupied him seriously for a while and suddenly, unexpectedly, he smiled at me. 'Old Prune? She's all right.'

'You've known her a long time?'

'Forever. Since primary school.' Again he made it sound like a question.

'Did you fancy her at all?'

'Prune? Like I've known her since we were young. We were just friends. Mates. Dad used to pick her up on the school run and I'd see her every day. Mates. That's all we were. Right?'

'They say you sent her messages.'

'Why would I want to send her messages when I saw her all the time? There wouldn't have been a whole lot of point in it.'

'So you didn't send her e-mails?'

He was working again with his knife on the edge of the table. 'You believe I did, don't you?'

'I never said that.'

'Like everyone believes I did.'

'Not everyone.'

'Who doesn't then?'

'I told you. I don't. I'm in no hurry to believe anything. Now, as I told you, I assume you are innocent.'

He stopped sawing then, having done the edge of the table little visible damage. He put the knife down and looked at me. 'No one's said that to me before. You going to speak up for me? Like in Court?'

'If you want me to.'

'There's nothing much you could do.'

'Oh yes there is. I'd see if they could prove it.' He was silent then and I felt I had to say, 'Your parents think you might want someone younger.'

He flicked the knife with a finger and spun it as it lay on the table. I remembered, at his age, spinning knives to make decisions or answer questions, even to point out a guilty party. It came to rest pointing at me.

'All right then.' He was looking at me, as though accepting an inevitable conclusion. 'You'll do, right? You're cool.'

'Thank you very much.' I looked at old Beazely and confirmed my engagement. 'That's settled then.'

'Is that all?' Ben looked longingly back to the table where the other student waiters and waitresses were laughing, or blowing across the top of a bottle to produce a strange boom. None of them, so far as I knew, was on bail awaiting trial. Ben wanted to get away to join them, I thought, and not to go home.

'For the moment. Come and see me in London, and don't vanish this time. You can send Mr Beazely an e-mail, just to confirm you'll be there.'

'All right then.' Ben couldn't wait to get up. 'Thank you very much.' It was an automatic thank you, his mother must have taught him to say it when he went to his first party. 'Thank you very much for having me.' He was not so very much older when it was a thank you for doing his case of harassment and assault.

'Just one more question.' I looked up at the young man who seemed, in many ways, still a child. 'Do you like poetry?'

'What do you mean?' He looked puzzled and I had to explain.

'Stuff in short lines. It rhymes quite often. Do you read it ever?'

'Not really. I'm not bothered with it.' He still looked longingly towards his friends.

'But you read some at school?'

'At school, yes. Most of it's boring.'

'Have you read Yeats, for instance?'

'Yeats? Never heard of him. Sorry, I've got to go now.' And he was away, back in his own world, with the young people of the college who found poetry boring and helped out at Il Paradiso in the evenings.

'It's hopeless though, isn't it? All the e-mails have got his name on them, for God's sake,' Beazely said, as we stood on the windy platform of Hartscombe station waiting for the last train to London. 'They all came from his machine.'

'He called her "Prune",' I remembered.

'What's that got to do with it?'

'If you nursed a secret, powerful lust for a girl, so strong that you bombarded her with passionate and sexually explicit e-mails, if you were tormented with such urgent longings, do you think you'd call her "Prune"?'

Beazely frowned, puzzled. Clearly I had invited him to speculate on an alien world, a territory far from his quiet, orderly life as a country solicitor. 'I still think we're on a loser. Is this Prune business your only point?'

'No,' I told him. 'Not quite the only one.'

It was about two in the morning when I undressed in the bathroom, climbed into my pyjamas and fitted myself into my side of the bed as far as possible from the sleeping Hilda.

'Rumpole,' her voice boomed out of the darkness, 'where do you think you've been?'

'I'm not sure. Probably dinner at the Ivy with a couple of starlets and then to Stringfellow's for the lap dancing. Oh, and I caught a bit of a cold playing chemmy. We'll have to take out a second mortgage.'

'Absolute stuff and nonsense! You tell as many lies as your clients. It must be catching.'

The voice of She Who Must Be Obeyed died away into the night. I had a momentary vision of a young girl, gazing up to heaven in mixed terror and joy, as a god, disguised as a swan, swooped down to ravish her. And then I, too, fell asleep.

'Naturally we want to be with him when he sees you, Mr Rumpole.'

'It's worried his mother almost to death.'

'It's worried you too, darling. I told you, Mr Rumpole, Chris treats him exactly as though he was his own son.'

Beazely the solicitor, looking unusually embarrassed, had brought the Swithins to my room.

'I can understand exactly how worried you are.' I started to pour a little oil on the troubled parents who appeared outraged.

'He's given us such an incredibly hard time for years. And now this. Have you no idea what we are going through?'

'I'm sure it's been horrible,' I hastened to reassure Chris. 'So why not take a little time off. Drop into a cinema. Have tea at a posh hotel. I just need to see my client alone. Otherwise he might be reluctant to say things you'd find hurtful.'

'Believe me, Mr Rumpole,' Chris gave me a sad little smile, 'he's perfectly capable of saying things we find hurtful to our faces. He's quite prepared to tell his mother she's fat, or me that I'm drunk when I just happen to open another bottle of wine at dinner.'

'Then I ask you to leave to save yourselves further pain.'

Hermione, with a sigh of resignation, moved towards the door. Chris followed her with displeasure. 'I suppose you'll allow us to attend our son's trial?' he said. 'That'll be far the most painful moment for us.'

'Of course I want you to be there. I'm sure,' I told Chris,

'that you'll be ready and willing to give evidence of Ben's good character.'

As soon as they left me, the telephone rang. A miracle had taken place and the werewolf was downstairs. I told Henry to bring him up as soon as his mother and Chris were clear of the building. Then I opened the brief and read the last document, an e-mail from our client to Beazely. It was headed 'chimes@fishnet.co.uk and the message, which I took a minute to decode, read 'HOPE 2CUB4 5PM 2MORROW'. It was signed with nothing but a smiling face which appeared, together with the address at the top of the document, on all the messages which were the subject of the prosecution case.

Ben Swithin had dressed down for the occasion, wearing jeans with ink writing on the knees, a baggy sweater with holes in it and trainers that might have been used for a marathon run through mud. He looked even younger than usual, a face unmarked by the years, a contrast to the carefully, perhaps expensively preserved good looks of his mother and step-father.

So I turned from the face of innocence to the pile of printed-out e-mails which dealt with an encyclopaedia of sexual fantasies, the penetration of every orifice, the ritual humiliations to be inflicted on the innocent Prune, a girl doing her A-levels at Hartscombe college. The language was constantly obscene, frequently ugly but, from time to time, as I had suggested to Chris, unexpectedly poetic. The werewolf read through them and appeared genuinely shocked. 'That,' he said with all the outrage of youth, 'is disgusting! Whoever wrote that needs locking up.'

However, Ben admitted that the messages were headed by his e-mail address and that he used the name 'Chimes'. 'Dad suggested that when he gave me the computer. It was a sort of joke about the Chimes of Big Ben. He thought it was like a clever idea so I went along with it. "Fishnet" is my provider.'

'So they all seem to come from you. Did you write them?'

'I never even heard,' he was looking at me steadily, 'of doing half these things to anybody.'

So we went through the dates and times the messages were sent. The times were late at night and Ben tried to remember which dates he was at home, or when he worked very late at the restaurant and stayed with friends, sleeping on other people's floors in Hartscombe. The task of trying to get Ben and his friends to remember dates and places with any accuracy whatever was one I was happy to leave to old Beazely, who had read the e-mails with a certain detachment, even going so far as to say after the werewolf had left us, 'I never saw any point in bondage, but there are one or two things in here I might suggest to my wife Avril. She used to be a bit of a goer in her day.'

Before we parted, I asked him to get hold of that persistent sleuth Fig Newton, and get him to keep a discreet watch with a view to satisfying my curiosity about certain aspects of our case.

Unlike Beazely, I found nothing in the documents I could possibly have suggested to Hilda who, as far as I knew, would not care to be a receptacle for honey. When I told her that I was defending a boy accused of bombarding a schoolgirl with obscene messages, she looked at me as though she had always known I followed a sordid and debased profession, and announced that she would be off to visit her old schoolfriend Dodo Mackintosh in Cornwall. 'I don't want to be about, Rumpole, while you're reading disgusting things, even to yourself. I'll enjoy a breath of fresh air in Lamorna Cove.'

Some nights later, I was discussing the wear and tear of

married life with Claude Erskine-Brown in Pommeroy's when Soapy Sam Ballard joined us in his new companionable ex-Bonzo mode. I told them both that my wife was fleeing to Land's End rather than be near me when I was reading erotic material.

'Does that mean,' Ballard looked hopeful, 'that your flat will be empty?'

'Not altogether empty. I'll be there.'

'Oh, I don't mind about you,' our Head of Chambers was kind enough to say. 'I was planning a little gathering. Just a few old friends. And we're looking for a venue.'

'What about the desirable family home in Belsize Park?'

'Wouldn't do at all. My wife wouldn't entertain the idea. Can we gather at yours? Of course you'd be very welcome to join us.'

'There's just one condition.' I was determined to sell the mansion flat for a high price. 'Are small cigars permissible in my room in Chambers from now on?'

'Oh, I suppose so.' The new, reconstituted, ex-Bonzo Ballard, the character who pined for his youth and gazed longingly at girls' bottoms, gave his permission and we had a deal.

There are certain cases undertaken by a criminal defender in which, on entering Court, you feel you've stepped into a giant refrigerator into which you're shut, freezing, for the rest of the trial. The cold winds of disapproval howl at you from all sides and every time you stand up you feel as if you are clearly identified as a septic sore on the body of the nation, closely related to the alleged sex offender in the dock. Such was my feeling when I entered the Crown Court, His Honour Judge

Denis Wintergreen presiding, sitting at Hartscombe in the Home Counties.

The Swithins were, of course, there, sitting in front of me, holding hands to support each other in what everyone realized was the final and bitterest blow struck by the evil teenager in the dock. The prosecution was in the friendly hands of the owlish Adrian Hoddinot, who at least had the decency not to look at me as though I were a serial rapist who happened to have a wig on his head.

Adrian opened the case and read out some of the most horrific e-mails to a stony-faced Judge who wouldn't have minded saying 'Guilty' right away. I asked him to read one more, page thirty-two of the bundle. Obligingly the prosecutor read, without emotion:

How can your terrified, vague fingers push my feathered glory from your loosening thighs? I will produce a shudder in your loins. Ours will be an historic moment when I, the great bird God, swoop down on you.

'Is there any particular reason why you want that one read, Mr Rumpole?' Wintergreen was a hefty, square-jawed Judge who had played rugby football for his country. He clearly thought that any defence of this werewolf in the dock would be nothing but an unnecessary waste of time.

'The words don't suggest anything to you, Your Honour?' I asked him.

'Nothing more than that whoever wrote them must have a peculiarly filthy mind.'

'That may not be fair to the particular author concerned.'

'That will be a matter for the Jury to decide, Mr Rumpole.'

'Exactly! So wouldn't it be best if Your Honour would refrain from comment until that time comes?'

'Continue with your opening, Mr Hoddinot.' Winter-green cut me dead and looked only at the prosecution. 'Perhaps we may be spared any further interruption from Mr Rumpole.' I'd have to face it, relations between me and the learned judge during this trial were not going to be friendly.

Prunella Haviland gave evidence. She had received all the e-mails. At first she tried to ignore them, but finally she told her parents and, when the messages kept on coming, they told the police. She stood in the witness box, a slim, sensible, pretty girl with clear features who gave her evidence calmly, sensibly and without embarrassment. You could see her, when the bloom of her youth had faded a little, as a loyal wife and, like Hermione, a frequenter of charity dinners and coffee mornings in Hartscombe.

'What effect did receiving all these messages have on you – on your state of mind?' Adrian asked.

'Well, to start with I didn't take them too seriously. But then I got worried, of course. I didn't want to go out on my own at night. Particularly after what happened down the passage off the market square . . .'

'Tell the Jury about that.'

So she told them, clearly, calmly, without exaggeration. She'd been to American Pie, the club in Thames Street. She left early because she had an essay to finish, but it was dark when she walked through the market square and even darker when she got to the narrow passage I'd found with Mr Beazely on our way to the station. She was walking quickly, already nervous in the dark, when she felt strong arms gripping her from behind and a quick, damp kiss on the back of her neck. She struggled and freed herself. Then she ran, fast and without turning back, until she reached the main road.

'You never saw his face?'

'No.'

'So you've no idea who he was?'

'I couldn't tell. He was just someone strong. He had a smell. I noticed that.'

'What sort of smell?'

'An aftershave. Machismo Three. I know it because my dad uses it. It's quite a nice smell, really.'

'But it wasn't nice being attacked in the dark alley?'

'Please don't ask leading questions.' I rose wearily to my feet.

'Have you some objection, Mr Rumpole?' Wintergreen could see me standing there with my mouth open – I don't know what His Honour thought I was doing.

'My learned friend asked a question which suggests an answer to the witness. That's called a "leading question" and I object to it.' I explained, to the best of my ability, the situation to the rugger-playing Judge.

'I will allow the question.' And His Honour asked it again, from the bench. 'Was it nice being attacked in that way, Miss Haviland?'

'No, Sir. It certainly was not.'

'"It certainly was not."' His Honour repeated the words loudly and clearly, just in case we had the odd deaf juror, as he wrote them down. And then he asked, as though expecting the answer 'No', 'Have you any questions of this witness, Mr Rumpole?'

'Just a few, my Lord.' I turned to Prunella and became, I hope, Rumpole at his most gentle, charming and polite. 'Miss

Haviland, I realize how upsetting these dreadful messages must have been to you. I suppose, at first, all you knew was that they were from someone called "Chimes"?'

'Yes. That's right.'

'Thank you. When did you discover that "Chimes" was in fact Ben Swithin?'

'When my dad told the police. They found that out.'

'Was that after the attack in the dark passage?'

'It was after that, yes.'

'So when you were attacked, you didn't think it was Ben who was sending you these obscene messages.'

'I didn't know that. No.'

'So it might have been any man in the world who happened to use Machismo aftershave?'

'Well,' Prunella differed from the learned Judge in that she had a completely fair attitude to her case, 'I suppose that's right.'

'But now you know what you know,' the rugger player couldn't help joining in this scrum, 'who do you think attacked you?'

'I think it was Ben Swithin.'

'"I think it was Ben Swithin,"' His Honour repeated very loudly, for the benefit of the deaf juror, as he wrote it down. Then he turned on me, careful to sound more in sorrow than in anger.

'Mr Rumpole. Hasn't this young lady suffered enough?'

'She has certainly suffered. I quite agree with that.'

'Then why add to her suffering by making her go over all these painful matters again? Can't you leave it at that, Mr Rumpole?'

'Your Honour is telling me I shouldn't cross-examine?'

'Not to cause this young girl pain, Mr Rumpole.'

'Then how about the pain inflicted on the young boy in the dock if he's convicted of a crime he didn't commit?'

'Naturally, when it comes to sentence I shall have regard to the amount of embarrassment caused to Miss Haviland at the trial.'

'You mean you intend to punish my client for the way I choose to conduct his case?'

'Mr Rumpole, that was an outrageous remark!'

'Then it was very like Your Honour's intervention.'

The learned Judge was staring at me, strongly tempted, I believe, to hurl himself from the bench and tackle me low. So I decided to take preventive action. As I was considering this, I saw Chris Swithin writing a note which he turned and handed up to me. Before reading it, I assured the not-so-learned Judge, 'If Your Honour stops my cross-examination, I shall have to ask for an adjournment so I can go straight to the Court of Appeal.' It was this threat that tackled the Judge, perhaps temporarily stunned him. The Appeal Court had spoken unkindly of recent Wintergreen summings up. 'Slipshod,' they had said. 'Misleading . . . Clearly not thought out.' As he picked himself up and regained consciousness, I read the note from Chris.

'Don't ask any more questions!' was what my client's stepfather said. I squashed his note into a small ball and dropped it on the floor as the Judge kicked the case into touch. 'You may cross-examine, Mr Rumpole. Whether your questions help your case is quite another matter.'

'Miss Haviland, have you known Ben for a long time?'

'We were at primary school together.'

'And at secondary school. And then you were getting ready for A-levels at Hartscombe College together.'

'That's right.'

'At any time at all, when you were with Ben, has he done anything you would complain of ?'

'Not that I remember.'

'Did you like him, until you got these messages?'

'He was all right. I mean, well, yes. We were good friends.'

'Did he ever try to kiss you?'

'I was not one of his girlfriends.'

'So he never kissed you?'

'Not that I remember.'

'Or try to?'

'I don't think so, no.'

'So when you were told that he'd written these e-mails, did it come as a complete surprise to you? Were you amazed?'

'Yes.' She gave a sudden smile, which did more for the defence than I'd managed to do all that day. 'To be honest, I was gobsmacked.'

I invited the friendly prosecutor to lunch at Il Paradiso, where we enjoyed a quick cutlet Milanese and a glass or two of Chianti red. 'Terrible thing,' the manageress told us as she poured the wine. 'I can't imagine Ben doing a thing like that. You never know, do you?'

'No,' I agreed with her. 'You never know.'

When she had gone, I raised a glass to Adrian Hoddinot. 'I've thought of a scheme, old darling,' I told him. 'It'll bring the case to a fairly quick conclusion so you can spend more time with your Great Dane.'

'Good old Ophelia.' Adrian seemed attracted to the idea. 'She deserves a day out in the country.'

'Very well. Here's what I plan to do. And I do need your cooperation . . .' Then I told Adrian Hodinott all I knew.

★

It was mid-afternoon before I got round to opening my case. I reminded the Jury about the presumption of innocence and the burden of proof, giving such matters an importance which His Honour might seek to minimize. Then I announced that I would call young Ben's stepfather first, as he was a busy man and anxious to get away. To the Judge's disappointment, prosecuting counsel raised no objection and Chris Swithin made his way to the witness box. I thought he walked a little unsteadily, but there was only the slightest slur in his voice as he took the oath. I had noticed, when we sat in his study waiting for the werewolf's non-arrival, that he had shown such slight lack of focus after yet another large brandy, and came to the conclusion that he had lunched not wisely but too well. However that might have been, he turned respectfully to the Judge and answered my questions in clear, ringing tones. I got through the essential preliminaries, then asked him his view of Ben's character.

'Difficult, I have to say. Extremely difficult. At times quite impossible.'

It wasn't what you might expect from a character witness, but it delighted the Judge, who repeated ' "At times impossible" ' in a loud voice before he wrote it down.

'He's taken your name. He agreed to that, at least?'

'His mother asked him. He never thanked me for it. Well, I've learned not to expect thanks from Ben.'

'And I think he adopted your suggestion of calling himself "Chimes" on his e-mails. As in the chimes of Big Ben.'

'I thought he might enjoy the joke.'

'And apparently he did?'

'He never said so.'

' "He never said so." ' The Judge gave utterance like a ventriloquist's doll worked from the witness box.

'I want to ask you about his computer.'

'I bought it for his sixteenth birthday.'

'I bought it, for his birthday.' Big Sir Echo was the learned Judge.

'It is in his bedroom, which is, unusually, downstairs?'

'He was making such a noise coming up to bed at all hours, we moved him down to what had been the farm office. We had it decorated nicely for him.'

'"Decorated nicely."' The Judge again.

'Does that room have windows opening on the back of the house? I mean, it's possible to see into it by standing behind the building?'

'Yes, it is.'

'Have you ever used Ben's computer yourself?' I asked the question lightly, in all innocence, but it got an angry reply.

'Never. I told you. I bought it for him. I have all my own IT equipment in the converted barn. That's where I run my business. To keep the family going.'

'Let me ask you this. You know Prunella Haviland. I think you used to pick her up on the school run?'

'I did, yes, before Ben caused all this trouble. I thought she was an extremely nice girl.'

'I'm sure the Jury thought so too. Tell me, Mr Swithin, did you find her attractive?'

'Mr Rumpole,' the Judge looked like a referee who'd just been kicked on the shins by a delinquent player, 'I'm sure Mr Hoddinot will object to that question.'

'No objection, Your Honour.' I had briefed Adrian the prosecutor well, and he earned the Judge's frown of displeasure. Chris, however, spoke up, full of confidence. 'I'm perfectly prepared to answer the question. I think any man would find her extremely attractive.'

'You say "any man", Mr Swithin.' The Judge leaned forward graciously to the witness. 'Does that include any teenager?'

'It certainly does, Your Honour,' was the right answer. The Judge noted it down gleefully.

'I want you to look at the e-mails.' The bundle of print-outs was handed up to Chris Swithin. 'First of all, you have sworn that you never used Ben's computer?'

'He knew how to handle it before we got it. I never touched it, I've told you that on my oath, Mr Rumpole.'

'He's told you that, Mr Rumpole.' Judge Wintergreen was writing aloud.

'Then let's look at them. The first is one he sent to my Chambers before a conference. Do you see that?'

'Yes.'

'Do you see that it's written in a sort of code? The words 'see', 'to', 'you' and 'be' are indicated by capital letters or numbers.'

'That's the way young people send e-mails.'

'And yet in all the obscene e-mails to young Prunella no such code is used. All the words are written out properly in full.'

'I believe that is so.'

'You can take it from me it is so. Is that the way middle-aged people write e-mails?'

'Probably.'

'Do you use any of these abbreviations when you send e-mails?'

'I don't personally, no.'

'You spell and punctuate properly?'

'I like to do so.'

'You like to do so.' I glanced at the Jury box. Did I notice a stirring of interest? 'Let me turn to another subject. Were you pleased at Ben's fondness for poetry?'

Chris gave a small, bitter smile. 'Ben has no time for poetry whatever, I'm sorry to say.'

'Doesn't he even know the names of the major poets?'

'I don't think he does.'

'You yourself have a fine collection of books of poetry in your study. All arranged in alphabetical order from Arnold to Yeats.'

'I read English at Cambridge. I'm greatly moved by fine poetry.'

'And you admire the great poets of the last century, T. S. Eliot and W. B. Yeats, of course?'

'Of course I do.'

'Mr Rumpole,' the Judge put his oar in, 'are you wasting the time of my Court with this literary excursion? I'm sure Mr Hoddinot would think so.'

'I have no objection at all, my Lord.' Adrian the prosecutor disappointed His Honour again.

'So far as you know, the name Yeats would mean nothing to young Ben?'

'He's said that your client has no interest in poetry, Mr Rumpole,' Wintergreen reminded us.

'I know he has. Such a pity. Ben missed that beautiful lyric, 'Leda and the Swan'. I'm sure you have it well in mind, Mr Swithin.' The witness, for once, was silent, and I thought I saw for the first time on that handsome, lightly suntanned face, a hint of fear.

'Some of you may know the legend, Members of the Jury,' I told them. 'The girl Leda was raped by the King of the Gods, who disguised himself as a swan for the purpose. This

is how Yeats described it.' I opened a book which had nothing
to do with the law and read aloud,

> 'A sudden blow: the great wings beating still
> Above the staggering girl, her thighs caressed
> By the dark webs, her nape caught in his bill,
> He holds her helpless breast upon his breast.
>
> How can those terrified vague fingers push
> The feathered glory from her loosening thighs?
> And how can body, laid in that white rush,
> But feel the strange heart beating where it lies?
>
> A shudder in the loins engenders there
> The broken wall, the burning roof and tower
> And Agamemnon dead.'

The words rang and resonated in the stuffy courtroom.
Then I asked the witness to read out the relevant e-mail. He
seemed to have some difficulty finding the page, and further
difficulty in reading it out; but, in the end, he had no choice
but to do so.

'How can your terrified vague fingers push my feathered
glory from your loosening thighs? I will produce a shudder in
your loins. Ours will be an historic moment when I, the great
bird God, swoop down on you.'

'Did you send that e-mail to Prunella, Mr Swithin? Were
you Jupiter hoping, one day, she might be your shuddering
girl?'

The answer came back as a blustering question. 'What on
earth are you suggesting?'

'I don't know whether it was just because you enjoyed
sending erotic messages to a pretty young girl, or because you

wanted revenge on a stepson you'd grown to hate. Perhaps it was for both reasons. But you sent these e-mails, didn't you, Mr Swithin?'

'Mr Rumpole,' the Judge was equally outraged at this suggestion, 'you've called this witness as to character. You have no right to cross-examine him. I've been waiting for the prosecution to object.'

'Perhaps my learned friend,' I suggested as politely as possible, 'thinks the Jury are entitled to an answer. Perhaps I should explain this to Your Honour. That last E-mail was sent only three weeks ago. Just before this trial.'

'Which I regard as an act of gross contempt.' The Judge clung to his brief authority.

'That may be so. It's dated midnight on the seventeenth, a Friday night, when my client was enjoying a staff party in an Italian restaurant. I shall be calling a witness, a Mr Newton, an enquiry agent who observed Mr Swithin in my client's bedroom, operating young Ben's computer.'

It was then Chris began to shout. 'Ben! He's a pathological liar! He always has been! Werewolf! That's what we call him. He's an animal! No, worse than that! Animals have some dignity. He's evil! He's wrecked our marriage. He's . . .'

'Mr Swithin.' The Judge, at least, was calm. 'I have to warn you that you needn't answer any question that's likely to incriminate you.'

'Very well.' I saw what Chris was like then. He was like a small child, caught out in an act of pointless destruction. 'I won't answer.'

'Then perhaps you'll tell us this,' I said. 'A simple question, about the delightful aftershave I saw in your bathroom. What's it called – some dashing masculine title, like, perhaps, Machismo Number Three For Men?'

It was then that it happened, too quickly and far too unexpectedly for the Court usher dozing in his chair, or the officer in the dock, to give chase. Chris Swithin left the witness box with a turn of speed that recalled the days when he had won the hundred yards for his Cambridge college, and was out of the Town Hall and pushing his way through the crowd at the Craft Fair in the market square. No one recognized him when he grabbed the rail of a moving bus, or knew what happened when he got off at the next country stop. Were his business contacts clever enough to get him out of the country? Would he, some day, be extradited from southern Spain in a case of harassment? Perhaps not. All I know is that he was never seen again by his wife and family in Hartscombe.

When, on the excellent Adrian Hoddinot's application, the teenage werewolf was released from the dock and the prosecution dropped, I said goodbye to him outside the Court. Hermione, in tears, had her arms around him, holding him tightly with a mother's love. But he was the one who was doing the comforting.

I had a pub dinner that night (at the Trout Tickler beside the river) with Beazely and his wife Avril. She was a gentle, grey-haired woman with such a twinkle in her eyes that I wondered what, if any, new experiences she had been introduced to. It was late when I got home to the flat and as I went up the stairs I heard a noise, a cacophony of over-loud music. Was some new arrival in the building giving a party, a rare event in the tomb that was Froxbury Mansions? When I opened the front door, the noise enveloped me and rattled my brains.

It was in the sitting-room that it was going on. I remembered whom I'd lent a key to while Hilda was in

Cornwall, far away from the corruption of the e-mails. Owen Oswald from Wales was on drums, other Pithead Stompers were blowing and scraping hell out of a saxophone, a clarinet and a double bass. In the centre of it all, in his shirt sleeves and slapping a guitar, Bonzo Ballard was calling loudly on some unknown baby to light his fire.

I went into the kitchen and opened a bottle of Château Thames Embankment. How long would it be, I wondered, before these middle-aged men grew up and forgot the girls they might have known in the past? Lacking Hilda's determination, I couldn't turn them out. I poured myself a large glass and hoped for sleep.

Rumpole Rests His Case

'Members of the Jury. This case has occupied only ten days of your lives. In a week or two you will have forgotten every detail about the dead budgerigar, the torn-up photograph of Sean Connery, the mouldering poached egg on toast behind the sitting-room curtain and the mysterious cry (was it a call for help, as the prosecution invite you to believe, or the delighted shriek produced by a moment of sexual ecstasy?) which could be heard issuing from 42B Mandela Buildings on that sultry and fatal night of July the twenty-third. All this has been but a part, a fleeting moment perhaps, of your lives, but for the woman I represent, the woman who has endured every scrap of innuendo, scandal and abuse the almighty Crown Prosecution Service can dredge up, with the vast resources of the State at their disposal, for her this case represents the whole of her future life. That and nothing less than that is at stake in this trial. And it is her life I now leave, Members of the Jury, in your hands, confident that she will hear from your foreman, in the fullness of time, the words that will give the remainder of her life back to her: "Not Guilty!" So I thank you for listening to me, Members of the Jury. I rest my case.'

The sweetest moment of an advocate's life comes when he

sits down after his final speech, legs tired of standing, shirt damp with honest sweat, mouth dried up with words. He sits back and a great weight slides off his shoulders. There's absolutely nothing more that he can do. All the decisions, the unanswered questions, the responsibility for banging up a fellow human being, have now shifted to the Judge and the Jury. The defence has rested and the Old Bailey hack can rest with it.

As I sat, relaxed, and placed my neck comfortably against the wooden rail behind me, I removed the wig, scratched my head for comfort, and put it on again. As I rested, I looked for a moment at His Honour Judge Bullingham, an Old Bailey Judge now promoted to trying murders. To call them trials is perhaps to flatter the learned Judge, who conducts the proceedings as though the Old Bailey were a somewhat prejudiced and summary offshoot of the Spanish Inquisition. One of my first jobs as a defending counsel in the present case was to taunt and tempt, by many daring passes of the cape and neat side-steps in the sand, the bellowing and red-eyed bull to come out as such a tireless fighter on behalf of the prosecution that the Jury began to see him as I did. They might, perhaps, acquit my client because an ill-tempered Judge was making it so desperately clear that he wanted her convicted.

But who had killed the budgerigar, a bird which, it seemed, had stood equally high in the regard of both the husband and the wife? It was as I toyed with this question, in an increasingly detached sort of way, that I closed my eyes and found not darkness but a sudden flood of bright golden light into which the familiar furnishings of Court Number One at the Old Bailey seemed to have melted away and vanished. Then I saw a small black dot which, rushing towards me like a shooting star, grew rapidly into the face of His Honour Judge Bullingham, who filled the landscape wearing the complacent expression of a man about to pass a sentence of life imprisonment. Then I heard a voice, deeper and more alarming than that of any clerk of the Court I had ever heard before, saying, 'Have you reached a verdict on which you all agree?' 'We have,' some faint voice answered. 'Do you find the defendant Rumpole guilty or not guilty?' But before the answer could be given, the great light faded, and Bullingham's face melted away with it. There was a stab of pain in my chest, night fell and I became, I suppose, unconscious.

Undoubtedly, this was a dramatic way of ending a closing speech. Mrs Ballard, known round the Bailey as Matey, was soon on the scene, as I understand it loosening my collar and pulling off my wig. The prosecutor rose to ask His Honour what steps he wished to take in view of the complete collapse of Mr Rumpole.

'He's not dead. I'm sure of that.' Bullingham declined to accept the evidence. 'He's tried that one on me before.' This was strictly true, when, many years before, the stubborn old Bull dug his heels in and refused an adjournment, so I had to feign death as the only legal loophole left if I wanted to delay the proceedings.* I put on, as I thought, a pretty good performance on that occasion. But this was no gesture of theatrical advocacy. Matey made the appropriate telephone call. An ambulance, howling with delight, was enjoying its usual dangerous driving round Ludgate Circus. Strong men in uniform, impeded by offers of incompetent help from the prosecution team no doubt thankful to see the back of me,

---

* See 'Rumpole and the Last Resort'.

rolled me out of my usual seat and on to a stretcher. So I left Court (was it for the last time?) feet first.

'I know what this is,' I thought as I looked upon the vision of hell. My chest was still crunching with pain. There was a freezing draught blowing scraps of torn-up and discarded paper across the lino, and a strong smell composed of equal parts rubber and disinfectant. I saw some shadowy figures, a mother with a child on her lap, a white-faced girl with staring eyes and a scarlet mouth, an old man, his tattered coat tied with string, who seemed to have abandoned all hope and was muttering to himself, a patient Chinese couple, the woman holding up a hand swathed in a bloodstained bandage. They all sat beneath a notice which read: 'Warning. The average waiting time here is four and a half hours.' It seemed a relatively short period measured against eternity. If this place wasn't hell, I thought, it was, at least, some purgatorial anteroom.

When I had opened my eyes I had found myself staring at the ceiling, yellow plaster mysteriously stained, a globe surrounding a light in which, it seemed, all the neighbourhood insects had come to die. Then I realized, with a sudden pang, that I was lying on some particularly hard surface. It felt like metal and plastic and I was more or less covered with a blanket. Then a vision appeared, a beautiful Indian girl with a clipboard, wearing a white coat and a look of heavenly confusion. Perhaps this wasn't hell after all.

'Hello, Mr Robinson. Are you quite comfortable?'

'No.' I still had, so it seemed, retained the gift of speech.

'No, you're not comfortable?'

'No, and I'm not Mr Robinson either.'

'Oh. So that's all right then.' She made a tick somewhere

on her clipboard and vanished. I missed her but could no longer worry. I stirred with discomfort and went back to sleep.

When I woke up again, it must have been much later. The windows which once let in faint daylight were now black. The old man who had once sat quietly was now wandering round the room, muttering complaints and, from time to time, shouting 'Vengeance is mine!' or 'Up the Arsenal!'. There was a clattering as of a milk cart parking, and a formidable machine was wheeled up beside me, a thing of dials and trailing wires steered by a young man this time, also in a white coat. He had a large chin, gingery hair and an expression of thinly disguised panic. He also had another clipboard which he consulted.

'Ted Robinson?'

'No.'

'Collapsed in the workplace?'

'If you call the Old Bailey a workplace. Which I certainly never do.'

'All the same, you collapsed, didn't you?'

He'd got me there. 'Yes,' I had to admit. 'I collapsed completely.'

'All right, Mr Robinson. I'll just get you wired up.'

'But I'm really not . . .'

'You'll make it much easier for both of us if you don't talk. Just lie still and relax.'

I lay still as wires were fixed to me. I watched a line on a flickering screen which seemed to be on a perpetual downward curve. The stranger in the white coat was also watching. In the end the machine handed him a scrap of paper.

'Rest. A time in bed,' he told me. 'That's the best we can do for you.'

'But I haven't got a bed.'

'Neither have we.' He began to laugh, holding on to my arm as though he wanted me to join in the joke. 'Neither have we.' He repeated the phrase, as though to squeeze the last drops of laughter out of it. 'I expect someone, sometime, will do something about it. In the meantime, your job is to rest. Have you got that, Mr Rumpole?'

'You know my name?'

'Of course I do. We've got it written down. I don't know why you kept calling yourself Robinson all the time.'

No doubt the man worked unsociable hours. He wandered away from me in a sort of daze. Everything became terribly silent and, once again, I fell asleep despite the crunching pain.

My sleep was not undisturbed. Half awake and only a little conscious, I felt that I was on the move. I opened my eyes for a moment and saw the ceiling of a long passage gliding past. Then gates clanged. Was I at last going the way of too many of my customers? Was I being banged up? It was a possibility I chose to ignore until I felt myself rolled over again. I caught a glimpse of a kindly black face, the brilliant white teeth and hands pulling, in a determined way, at what was left of my clothing. Then I was alone again in the darkness, and I heard, like the waves of a distant sea, the sounds of low incessant snores, and the expulsion of breath was like the rattle of small stones on the beach as the waves retreat.

'I didn't bring you grapes, Rumpole. I thought you wouldn't want grapes.'

'No interest in grapes.' My voice, as I heard it, came out in a hoarse whisper, a ghostly shadow of the rich courtroom baritone which had charmed Juries and rattled the smoothest bent copper telling the smoothest lies. 'I'm only interested in grapes when they've been trodden underfoot, carefully fermented and bottled for use in Pommeroy's Wine Bar.'

'Don't talk so much. That's a lesson you'll have to learn from now on, Rumpole.'

I looked at Hilda. She had smartened herself up for this hospital visit, wearing her earrings, a new silk blouse and smelling a great deal more strongly than usual of her Violetta Eau de Toilette.

'I thought you wouldn't want flowers, Rumpole.'

'No. You're right, Hilda, I wouldn't want flowers.' Plenty of time for flowers, I thought, later.

'Flowers always look so sick in a hospital.'

'That's right, of course. Most of us do!'

Conversation between myself and She Who Must Be Obeyed was flowing like cement. It wasn't that we were embarrassed by the presence of other men on the ward. The snorer, the tooth-grinder, the serial urinator had headphones glued to their ears, their heads nodding gently to the beat of the easy listening. The young man who had lost a kidney held the hand of his visiting girlfriend; they only spoke occasionally and in whispers. The other youngish man, perhaps in his thirties, brown-haired with soft, appealing eyes and a perpetually puzzled expression, lay in the bed next to mine. His was a face I recognized from newspapers and the television, and I knew his name was David Stoker and that he had been operated on as a result of gunshot wounds.

'Let this be a lesson to you, Rumpole,' Hilda went on remorselessly. 'You've got to give it all up.'

This was how she spoke to me at home and she made no effort to moderate her tone, although the much-bandaged Stoker was well within earshot.

'Give what up, Hilda? I don't really mind giving up

anything, so long as it's not small cigars or Pommeroy's very ordinary or the Bar.'

'That's the one!'

'Which one?'

'The Bar. That's what you've got to give up. Well, after this business it's perfectly obvious you can't go on with it. All these criminals you're so fond of defending will just have to go off to prison quietly, and about time too, if you want my opinion, Rumpole.'

'Of course I want your opinion, Hilda. But . . .'

'No "but" about it. I've spoken to the doctor here.'

'That was nice of you. How is he?'

'He's perfectly well, Rumpole. Which is more than can be said about you. It's your heart. You've put too great a strain on it. You do understand that, don't you?'

'Is that what he said?'

'His very words.'

'He called me Robinson.' I thought of the most likely explanation for this ridiculous verdict. 'He's seriously over-worked. I don't think, Hilda, you should attach the slightest importance to his evidence.'

'That woman you were defending when you passed out. Your last case, Rumpole. The woman who stabbed her hus-band. You got her off.'

'I know,' I said. 'They let me read the Sunday papers. The Jury found she didn't mean to stab him. She held the knife to keep him away and he stumbled and fell on it. That's what the Jury believed.'

'What you persuaded them to believe.'

'I have a certain skill, as an advocate.'

'A skill that'll finish you off, Rumpole, if you don't give it up entirely.'

'Anyway, he wasn't a particularly nice man. He wrung her budgerigar's neck.'

'Oh, well, then I suppose he deserved it.' She was easily persuaded. 'But now you've given it all up, you'll be able to enjoy life.'

'Enjoy life doing what?'

'Well, you can rest. Help around the flat. I've always thought we ought to go in for window boxes. If you make a good recovery you could help me with the shopping.' I couldn't think of a weaker incentive for a return to health. But I didn't say so. A silence fell between us and then she said, 'I bumped into Chappy Bowers the other day.'

'Who?' The name meant little to me at first.

'You must remember Chappy. He was in Daddy's Chambers when you joined. He didn't get much work. It was rather sad. He said he just couldn't bear spinning improbable stories for ungrateful people.'

'Then he clearly had absolutely no talent for the law.'

'He went into the City and did a number of jobs. Then he fell on his feet. They made him secretary of his local golf club. Chappy Bowers loves his golf.'

'And where did you bump into him – on the thirteenth green?'

'Don't be silly, Rumpole. He rang me up when he read about your collapse in the *Evening Standard*. He agrees with me that you must have a complete rest. It's the only answer.'

'Has he got any medical qualifications, this Chappy person?'

'Not that I know of, but he's truly understanding, and, what's more, he's asked me out for dinner.'

'Where to – the Club House?'

'Of course not. He knows this little place in Soho. Very intimate and excellent cooking. He's told me I'll adore Chez Achille . . . Good heavens!'

This last breathed, barely whispered exclamation arose from Hilda's observation of the bed next to mine. David Stoker had been called for an X-ray. He couldn't immediately get up and go. A thin chain, about eight foot long, was cuffed to his wrist and the wrist of an overweight screw who, dressed informally in a sweater and tracksuit trousers, sat at the end of David Stoker's bed, easy listening also fastened to his ears. The screw rose and this mini-chaingang left us.

'He's in chains, Rumpole!' Hilda couldn't get over it. 'That patient is in chains!'

'That's right.' I did my best to reassure her. 'He's not dangerous. It's just that he had his operation while awaiting trial and the prison hospital's full up. He's got a bit of previous form, I know. Apart from that he's not a bad sort of young fellow.'

'Good heavens!' Hilda repeated her prayer. 'What's he waiting trial for?'

'House-breaking by night, I think it is. Armed with a pistol.'

She looked at me then, and said, more in sorrow than in anger, 'You just can't keep away from them, can you, Rumpole? The criminal classes. You just can't keep away from them at all.'

'Mr Rumpole.' The voice in the darkness came from the chained man in the bed beside me. 'Was that your wife, Mr Rumpole?'

'What did you think?'

'Well, I hardly thought it was your girlfriend.' He laughed softly but I didn't join in his laughter. 'She's a member of the public, isn't she? All members of the public hate me for what they think I've done.'

'What have you done, exactly?'

'Only got shot up so badly I had to have two hours on the operating table. Only got pumped as full of lead as a fucking pencil. And for getting that done to me, I'll probably get four years. That's what they tell me my brief's thinking of, four to five he reckons. That's my youth gone, all that's left of it.'

'Who's this brief you speak of?'

'It's a Mr Erskine-Brown QC. He's a senior man.'

'QC? I've always thought those letters stand for "Queer Customer". If you've got Claude defending you, you might as well plead guilty. He'll probably do you a very nice plea in mitigation.' As soon as I'd said that I regretted it. It wasn't worthy of me. The onset of death, I thought, brings out the worst in you.

'I'm joking of course,' I told him. 'Claude Erskine-Brown is a man of considerable experience.' And I restrained myself from adding, 'Of opera.'

There was silence then. At last my neighbour spoke in a smaller voice. 'I always heard you were a fighter, Mr Rumpole.'

'Where did you hear that?'

'Round the Scrubs. When I was in there. They were talking about it.'

'You've got a bit of previous, haven't you?'

'Quite a bit, to be honest. I was a bad lad in my younger years. Before I decided to straighten myself out.'

'Why don't you two shut the fuck up.' It was the snorer, to whom I owed quite a few sleepless nights, sending us a message from the other side of the ward.

★

I had read enough, when I was alive and kicking, in the newspaper accounts of the shooting at Badgershide Wood to recall David Stoker's past, both as instigator and victim of the affair, and to be able to inform Hilda of my neighbour's problem. The next day he opened his locker and brought out a bundle of press cuttings, copies of the indictment and statements of evidence, so I was able to sit up in bed and read the details of the events which had led my neighbour to the operating table and would take him to my familiar hunting ground at the Old Bailey and, in all probability, to a long term of imprisonment.

Badgershide Wood, from what I found out about it, did its best to claim that it was still a country village, an island in the suburban sprawl that stretched from the north-west of London towards the Chiltern Hills. It had a small Norman church, a main street, two pubs, four antiques shops, a hair-dressing salon called Snippers and a Thai restaurant. In the middle of the village, larger and more imposing than the church, was a Georgian house which had been the home of the Dunkerton family for generations. The present heir, Major Ben Dunkerton, was the hero who had peppered Stoker with shots and confined him to bed in chains.

Major Ben Dunkerton, who succeeded in behaving like an eccentric but amiable country squire in what had, in fact, become a suburb of London, did a great deal to preserve Badgershide Wood's claim to be a rural community. He was old enough to have joined the army in the last years of the War and had been honourably wounded after D-Day as a very young officer. He stayed on in the army until he took over the family business and became the Chairman of a local firm of estate agents. During his long retirement he was a favourite customer at the Badger's Arms, had a kind word for everyone in the village street and penetrated more deeply into the countryside to shoot with his old friends. He fished in Scotland and, although childless and a long-time widower, gave a lavish party for all the Badgershide Wood children at Christmas. He was spoken of with great affection as a thoroughly good chap, one who enjoyed his malt whisky and still, God bless him, had an eye for the girls.

Major Dunkerton's account of the night of the fifth of March was a simple one. He'd gone upstairs to get ready for bed when he heard sounds of breaking glass and something knocked over in the kitchen. He kept a shotgun upstairs, since there had been a number of cases of armed robbery in well-known country houses. He loaded the shotgun and went downstairs, calling first at the kitchen, where he saw a pane of glass broken, a window forced open and crockery smashed. Someone had undoubtedly crawled in through the window. The light had been left on.

Then he crossed the hall to the library, which was also lit. The door was open and he could see someone standing by his desk, a man he had no difficulty in identifying as Stoker. As the intruder turned, the Major saw he had what looked like an old army pistol in his hand. Before Stoker could shoot, the Major fired the shotgun and he fell, as the Major thought at first, dead. Before he could fully examine the fallen body, there was a loud knocking at the front door. It was Doctor Jefferson who, on his way to his home next door, had heard the shot and, when the Major opened the door to him, saw what at first sight he also thought was a dead body.

The police and the ambulance were called. When it was discovered that the shots hadn't killed Stoker, the Major was, to quote Doctor Jefferson, 'in a terrible state of anxiety as to whether the wretched robber was going to live or die'. What was clear from the newspaper cuttings, however, was that the great British public couldn't care less about the fate of my neighbour in the ward, and Major Ben Dunkerton was a national hero. His right to defend his house against an armed intruder was trumpeted. 'MAJOR'S HOUSE HIS CASTLE'; 'HE GOT HIS SHOT IN FIRST'; '76-YEAR-OLD MAJOR SHOOTS FOR HIS LIFE'; 'ARMED THUGS BETTER NOT MESS WITH MAJOR BEN': such were the headlines in all the papers.

The Major was charged with unlawful wounding, grievous bodily harm and a firearms offence. It was clear that the press regarded his trial as a short preliminary before a triumphant acquittal and the receipt of a George Medal for bravery. Stoker, the armed robber, however, was sure to be sent to prison for a sizeable chunk of the foreseeable future, once he was well enough to leave hospital.

Stoker's statement told a very different story – and one which, in contrast to Major Ben's clear account, seemed hard to swallow. His childhood had been perfectly happy. The only child of an insurance salesman and a devoted mother, he had done well at school and seemed set for a decent job, a first home on a mortgage and holidays on the Costa Brava. He was only seventeen, however, when, in the course of a night's clubbing, he fell in with a group of boys a year or two older, who had graduated from nicking car radios and snatching unattended handbags to house-breaking. 'It's the excitement, Mr Rumpole,' Stoker told me during one of our many conversations. 'There's no drug, no drink you can take like it. Standing in someone else's place when you know anything you fancy is yours to pick up, and them snoring upstairs. All right, it's dangerous. That's what's exciting about it. Dangerous but so easy, sometimes I had a hard job not to laugh out loud.'

By the time he was twenty-five, Stoker had half a dozen convictions and got four years.

It was in prison that he began to write a wry, unselfpitying account of life in the nick and the memories of a housebreaker, which led, apparently, to his reform. His book was serialized in a Sunday paper. He became, in the public eye, the statutory reformed con, the hard man gone soft, who appeared on television chat shows, took part in *Any Questions* and was rung up to comment yet again on the latest Criminal Justice Act introduced by the New Labour Party. So, instead of coming out of prison with a few pounds and an irresistible temptation to return to crime, Stoker had a flat in now fashionable Hackney and a steady income from his writing and as an adviser to a spate of British gangster films. He was held up as an example of how prison can work and how a long dose of it produces a reformed citizen wanting to appear on *Newsnight*. Such hopes were dashed by the appearance of David Stoker, not answering the questions of the day but armed and having broken into an elderly stranger's house by night.

As I say, Stoker's explanation would have seemed way beyond the bounds of probability, even in the gangster films on which he gave advice. There was a girl named Dawn, once the girlfriend of one of his burgling mates, whom he had always fancied. They had met again by chance in a club round Notting Hill Gate and she had told him that she had tired of London and had a flat in a town near Badgershide Wood, where she had satisfied a long-held ambition to open a hairdressing salon. Now she had a thriving business offering up-to-the-minute hairdos to a large catchment area. So far so bad. Stoker's knowledge of the village, and the presence of a large and robbable house, was now explained.

From there on his story got stranger. He had, he said, met Major Ben Dunkerton before. Dawn was busy with a customer and he had gone for a walk in the woods, where an elderly man with a tweed cap and a walking stick came up to him and said he recognized him from the television.

'I've seen you around the village from time to time,' the Major said. 'Attractive place, isn't it?' And he added, with a particular emphasis, 'I'm sure it must have many attractions for you.'

Then he went on to be extremely complimentary to Stoker on his reform and his literary skills. 'Wouldn't your book make a tremendously exciting film?' the Major asked him, before mentioning a hugely famous, although also elderly, film director whom he said he had known 'since our National Service days', who would love to meet David. And so a meeting was arranged for one of the few nights when the director would be touching down in Badgershide Wood between Los Angeles and his current location in Morocco.

'Have to be a bit late, I'm afraid. Sam is having dinner with the money people. But he'll be back at my house around ten-thirty, if you'd like to call in for a nightcap?'

Stoker said he took all this in, including the Major's improbable demand for secrecy.

'Sam would hate there to be any sort of publicity about meeting you before a deal's done. So if you could keep quiet about all this, to everyone?'

'Of course.'

'Better not even tell your friend the hairdresser. You know how quickly these stories get about.'

'All right, I won't tell her. I'm going back to London tonight anyway.'

'So why not drive straight to my house tomorrow evening? You can park round the back. Not a word to anybody.'

Not unnaturally, Stoker was surprised at the complexity of these arrangements. 'Why are you doing all this for me?'

'Because I think, from what I've heard and read about you,' the Major told him, 'you're a decent lad that's doing his best to go straight, and I want to encourage you.'

Stoker put it down to being so used to obeying orders and having everything arranged for him in prison that he obeyed the Major's curious instructions. He drove down the next evening, straight from his flat in Hackney. He got to the Major's house at ten-twenty-five, parked behind it and walked round to ring at the front door.

Before he could touch the bell the door was opened by the smiling Major, who showed him into the study, a book-lined room. On the desk, carefully laid out on the blotter between the paperweight and a letter-opener, lay an old service revolver.

'Used to be mine in my army days. I brought it home when I was demobbed. I know you're interested in guns.'

'I never went tooled up,' Stoker said he assured the Major.

'Just feel it. Perfect balance, hasn't it? For an outdated weapon.'

Again obedient, Stoker picked up the pistol, felt its weight as directed and put it down as quickly as possible. 'I know Sam will want guns in his picture,' the Major said. 'By the way he's just gone upstairs for something. I'll go and hurry him up.'

The Major left then, but returned almost immediately. What happened next was, according to Stoker, quite inexplicable. As he turned to face the door, his host lifted a shotgun and fired. Stoker remembered a blow like a kick from a horse, a sudden and terrible pain, and then darkness – until he came to, bumping in the back of an ambulance in such agony that he wished he'd never woken up.

One other fact emerged from the mass of papers he'd handed me. Sam, the famous film director, was nowhere near England on the date of the shooting and, when asked, denied all knowledge of Badgershide or Major Dunkerton. All this proved was that either David Stoker or the Major was lying prodigiously. That was no help to either of them.

'Long time, Rumpole, such a very long time no see.'

When I first put on the whitest of white wigs, having joined the Chambers of C. H. Wystan, my wife Hilda's 'Daddy', there was, if I recollect, a rather chubby, smiling-for-no-reason young barrister, reduced to inarticulate jelly by appearing in Court for something really taxing, like fixing a date for a hearing. His career in the law had been short and unimpressive, but Chappy Bowers, as he rather liked to be known, had, as the climax of an apparently harmless and uneventful life, 'bumped into' Hilda after ringing her up because he'd heard of my collapse in Court. Unexpected and uninvited, he turned up and sat himself down in my visitor's chair just when my mind was full of strange and far more interesting business at Badgershide Wood. He still managed to look boyish in his grey-haired age. His face was round and chubby, his eyes blue and anxious to please and he had, over the years, become no more articulate.

'When we were, er . . . in Chambers together, I – well, what I mean is we – were both of us, what's the word? Umm . . . smitten by Hilda Wystan.'

'I suppose we were.' I didn't want to tell him that, from my point of view, I sometimes felt that the smiting had gone on for a lifetime.

'What I really came to, well . . . I mean, umm, what I came to . . . well, really, and in all honest truth, Rumpole, to say was that if anything should happen to you. And it's a big "if ".'

'No, it's not.' I couldn't help correcting him. 'It's not a big "if " at all. I collapsed in Court with a dicky ticker. I'm confined in the hospital block and have no idea when I'll get out of it. Any day, to be honest with you, I might lose my grasp of the twig.'

'Well, if that . . . Well if . . . Which umm – we profoundly . . . Well, not profoundly. What's the word?'

'Sincerely?'

'That's it, Rumpole! Trust you, old fellow. You always knew the right word. Sincerely.'

'That's the word you use when you don't mean what you're saying.'

'No? Not really? No! I do mean this. Of . . . umm. Of course I do. If, again I say *if*, you should drop off the . . . What was it, Rumpole?'

'Twig?' I suggested.

'Yes, if you should drop off the twig, Hilda knows she'd always have someone to look after her.'

'You mean her friend Dodo Mackintosh?'

'No, Rumpole.' Now the words came out in a rush. 'I honestly mean me.'

'You'd look after Hilda, if I turned up my toes?'

'It would be an honour and a privilege.'

'Then all I can say, Chappy, old darling, for the sake of

your health and sanity, is I'd better make an astonishing recovery.'

Conversation dried up then, until Chappy leant towards me and said in a penetrating whisper, 'That fellow in the next bed – looks, well . . . umm, chained up.'

'That's because he *is* chained up,' I explained. 'It's what they do to you nowadays if you get shot.'

When Chappy had gone back to his golf club, apparently unshaken in his desire to take care of She Who Must Be Obeyed, I asked Ted, the screw, to put the headphones on again for another dose of Petula Clark and asked the wounded suspect just a few more questions.

'You parked your car round the back of the house. Did you notice a kitchen window open?'

'It was quite dark.'

'A window broken?'

'I didn't notice.'

'Did *you* break a window?'

'I told you, I came in by the front door.'

'You say the Major was there waiting. He opened it for you.'

'He must have seen my car arrive.'

'You told me that.'

After that I gave my full attention to the evidence of the Scene of Crime Officer, with particular relation to finger-prints.

'Henry.' I was on the ward telephone to my clerk.

'Mr Rumpole! We heard you were taken really bad, Sir. It's good to hear you're still with us, as you might say.'

'As you might say, Henry, if you were in a particularly

tactless mood. Never mind. It's wonderful to hear your voice. Just like old times.'

'It's not about work, is it, Sir? Mrs Rumpole rang to say we weren't to worry you about work. She said you'd be resting from now on. It made me feel envious. Not much rest round Equity Court. Not for a clerk, there isn't.'

'It's not about my work. Actually, it's about someone else's work. Mr Erskine-Brown's got an attempted robbery case called Stoker.'

'The Badgershide Wood job? I'm afraid it's going to clash with a civil he's got. Personal Injury with real money to it. Claude's leading Mizz Probert in the crime.'

'Henry.'

'Yes, Sir?'

'Remind me to order the drinks in Pommeroy's if you let them clash. And go for the civil.'

'That's what I had in mind. But why exactly?'

'Who knows? I might be leading Mizz Liz in the Badgershide shooting business. Stranger things have happened.'

'You think Mrs Rumpole would allow it, Sir . . . ?'

'We'll wait and see if we've got any sort of defence. Oh, and get Bonny Bernard to give me a ring here, will you? The Princess Margaret ward. You have to sell your soul here to make an outside call.'

The system was that a telephone was wheeled to the side of your bed as though it was a cardiogram machine or materials for a blanket bath. If there was a call for you, it came after a short interval. If you wanted to make a call you had to wait a considerable time for the instrument, and also provide money to cover its cost. I had to pay out to call Henry, so I was relieved when Bonny Bernard's voice was wheeled towards me, with a selection of pills as an after-breakfast treat.

'You had a brief in a sensational shoot-out in an old-age pensioner's home and you sent it to Erskine-Brown?' I accused the man.

'I was planning it for you. But then we heard you'd left the Bar.'

'The Bar? I never left it. Left life perhaps, but the Bar? Never! Now listen, my old darling. It's very possible that Claude Queer Customer may not be able to do this case owing to the pressures of civil work in the Personal Injuries Department.'

'So we'll have to look elsewhere, then.'

'You may not have to look very far. The future depends, to a certain extent, on the evidence of the heart. All I ask is that you don't rush into any decisions. And there's one thing you can do.' I gave Bonny Bernard certain instructions and then I asked him if he'd like to speak to his client. 'He happens to be here beside me.'

'Mr Rumpole,' Bernard's question came in a horrified whisper, 'you're not in the nick, are you?'

'Don't worry, old darling. He's in hospital.'

I covered the mouthpiece and called to my neighbour, 'Would you like to speak to your solicitor?'

'No point, is there? He came to see me before you got here. Then he sent me all these papers. I could see it in his face. He didn't believe a word I said.'

'We'll talk to you later,' I told Bernard, 'when we've decided if there's a possible defence.'

'Can't you remember, Mr Rumpole, you're meant to rest . . .' My old friend started some form of protest and I put the phone down gently.

★

It happened a few mornings later when Stoker needed some minor surgery. He was wheeled away chained to his trolley and accompanied by his shadow, Ted, the ever-present screw. I saw another visitor enter the ward, a thin, hawk-like figure in a crumpled mackintosh carrying, like an angel in a painting, a stiff, upright bunch of white lilies as though to deck the top of a coffin. He sat in my visitor's chair, removed his hat, and Esmeralda, the cheerful Jamaican nurse we were always glad to see, relieved him of his flowers, promising to put them in water.

'Would you rather have had grapes, Mr Rumpole?'

'Grapes, lilies, it's all the same to me,' I told him. 'It's you I wanted to see, Fig. You're going to provide the key to my present problem.'

'Your heart?'

Did Ferdinand Ian Gilmour (known to us as Fig) Newton believe that I credited him with medical skills?

'Of course not. My heart can look after itself. It would, however, be greatly encouraged by a solution to the mystery of the Badgershide Wood shooting.'

'Is it a mystery, Mr Rumpole? In my paper it's just a decent citizen defending himself and his property.'

'Perhaps your paper doesn't know the half of it.'

'No? You may be right, Mr Rumpole. What's the other half, then?'

'That's exactly what I want you to find out. Hang around Badgershide Wood with your ears open. Find out all you can about the eccentric Major. Oh and there's a girl called Dawn something who works at Snippers the hairdressers.'

'You want her kept under twenty-four-hour observation? I'm afraid we're in for some inclement weather.' Fig sniffed gloomily, as though in anticipation of the cold he was likely to catch.

'Don't just observe her. Meet her. Taker her off to the Thai restaurant. Make her like you. Say that if she tells us all she knows, it just might help her wounded lover escape a lengthy sentence. Mention my name if you have to. Say that Rumpole is relying on her. No, better still, tell her that a hospital patient in chains thinks of her constantly.'

'I brought you a few grapes, Rumpole.'

'That was very thoughtful of you, Hilda.'

'Don't eat them all at once. They looked nice in the shop.' She Who Must pulled off a couple and chewed them thoughtfully. 'Not bad at all. Nice and juicy. Well now, Rumpole.' She looked at me with an eye born to command. 'I want you to make a complete recovery.'

'Anything you say, Hilda.' I had no intention of arguing with her. 'Your fancy man was here.'

'My what?'

'Your fellow. Your little bit on the side,' I might have said. Instead I stuck to 'Your friend Chappy Bowers. The one who took you out to a candlelit dinner. I hope you enjoyed it.'

'I did *not* enjoy it, Rumpole!'

'Veal escalope on the tough side, was it? Nasty collapse of the soufflé at . . . What was it called?'

'Chez Achille in Soho. The ladies' lavatory was down a long, damp staircase and far too near the kitchen, and I didn't find the tablecloth entirely clean.'

'And no candles?'

'Oh yes. There was a nasty guttering thing in an old wine bottle. The waiter was extremely familiar with Chappy and said, "Another of your girlfriends, Mr Bowers?" before we even got a glance at the menu.'

'Wasn't that rather a compliment?' The waiter, I thought, was laying it on with a trowel by putting Hilda in the 'girl-friend' category.

'Not to be called a girlfriend of Chappy's. I imagine they're a lot of old trouts.'

'Oh yes,' I nodded. 'Of course that's what they probably are.'

'I wouldn't want to be the "girlfriend", Rumpole, of any man who added up his bill.'

'Did Chappy do that?'

'Worse than that. They gave us each, Rumpole, a "selection of vegetables" on two small plates.'

'That was bad news?'

'I wasn't greatly impressed. We had a few bullet-hard potatoes, some green beans that were also undercooked, and three undersized carrots. Well, Chappy actually asked for a reduction because we hadn't eaten the potatoes.'

'On the tight side, as I remember. Always fumbled for his money when it was his turn at Pommeroy's.'

'He is the sort of man, Rumpole, who would check up on a woman's shopping list.'

I knew a great deal of the Rumpoles' income was frittered away on such luxuries as Ajax, kitchen rolls and saucepan scourers, but I would never have intruded on the sanctity of Hilda's list.

'So I want you to recover, Rumpole,' she went on. 'You may have your faults, but you don't argue about the selection of vegetables. So, what I'm trying to tell you is, I simply couldn't put up with a person like Chappy Bowers. I want you back round the house.'

'That is very encouraging, Hilda.'

'I hope you will agree to give up work entirely. That's the only way you're going to get well. It's so good your being here, where you can't spend your time worrying about crimes.'

I glanced at the prisoner in the next bed. He lowered the *Daily Beacon* slightly and closed one eye in a discreet wink.

I took the opportunity to discuss the Major with the customers in the Badger's Arms as well as the staff at the local garage and the owners of at least two of the antiques shops. On all sides he's spoken of as a hero who was acting in self-defence and to protect his property. There is no sympathy whatsoever for the client.

Fig Newton's reports never concealed the bad news, for which he has a particular relish. He went on:

The Major is admired as an amiable eccentric. 'His own man,' the landlord of the Badger's Arms told me. 'One of the old school. Friendly with everyone, likes his drop of Scotch and always got an eye for the ladies.' It's the landlord's opinion that the client, when he entered the Major's house, got exactly what he deserved. Several of the regulars in the Badger's Arms and the landlord said they had seen the client, whom they recognized from his photograph in the papers, on his visits to Snippers the hairdressers.

I myself called at Snippers on the pretext of a hair wash and trim, as the place is advertised as 'unisex'. Dawn Maresfield was engaged with another client and I was attended to by a 'trainee stylist'. I did, however, get the chance of a word with Miss Mares-field, and when I told her we were acting in the interests of David Stoker, she agreed to meet me after work. We fixed a rendezvous in the Pizza Palace of the Parallelogram Shopping Mall, about eight miles from Badgershide Wood. Her reason for choosing this venue was, she said, that 'people were talking'.

At my meeting with Miss Maresfield, I formed a favourable impression of her and think that, if the time should ever come, she'd make a good witness. She said she was very disappointed with David, who she thought had gone back to his old criminal ways and ruined his life. She was, however, extremely worried about his condition and, when pressed, said she would see him again, and I feel she retains her affection for him.

Her attitude to the Major was in marked contrast to the view of him held by all the other witnesses. When I first mentioned him she sighed heavily and said, 'Don't talk about him.' When I told her that he was what I wanted her to talk about, she said he'd been a pest, a nuisance, a bit of a joke at times, and at times a menace. I asked if that meant he had taken a fancy to her, and she said she would have described it as 'besotted'. He'd sent her flowers, presents, bits of jewellery that had belonged to his family which didn't suit her and she had no use for. She said she'd been out with him once or twice but she'd got tired of moving his hand off her knee. 'He even tried to stick his tongue down my throat in the car and would have if I hadn't clenched my teeth on him. At his age it is just ridiculous.' His letters to her became 'just disgusting', so she stopped opening them. Quite recently he'd telephoned her at work and told her he knew she'd marry him if it wasn't for that 'bloody little crook' he'd seen her with. She thought that when he said that he was probably drunk, because she'd never told him about Stoker and, as far as she knew, they'd never met. She never told Stoker about the Major's advances as she was afraid he'd go up to the big house and make a scene, which would do her no good: she relied on the Major's many friends of both sexes to get their hair styled at Snippers.

I don't know how much this helps and I am not clear at the moment what further steps I can take. I therefore await further instructions and I enclose my account, which includes travel expenses and a reasonable sum for entertaining at the Badger's Arms and the Pizza Palace in the Parallelogram Shopping Mall.

(signed) F. I. G. Newton. Member of the National Institute of Enquiry Agents.

I put down Fig's report and yes, I thought, we're ready for trial. I had a great deal to say and I could hardly wait for an opportunity to say it.

It was late, almost midnight, when I began my final speech. I made it to a Jury which included the snorer, the tooth-grinder and the serial urinator, who stayed in his bed during the greater part of it. I was sufficiently confident of my case to allow Ted the screw on duty to remove his earphones and listen from the public gallery. Quietly and, I believe, with perfect fairness, I outlined the prosecution case, the facts which had appeared in all the newspapers, the story of an outraged householder who was merely upholding the sacred principle that an Englishman's home is his castle.

'Now I come,' I spoke even more quietly, causing the Jury to listen attentively as I lured them into taking another and totally different view of the facts, 'to the case for the defence of David Stoker. The defence is not made easier by the fact that it is well known that he had committed offences in the past, indeed he has written about them and spoken about them on television. We are not trying him for his past offences, and you must be even more vigilant to see that he is not now, because of his past, convicted of a crime he didn't commit.

'The first thing that puzzled me was the report of the Scene of Crime Officer who was in charge of taking fingerprints.

There were, of course there were, Mr Stoker's fingerprints on the old army pistol on the library table, but, extraordinarily enough, Members of the Jury, *nowhere else*. In the light of that, let us consider how he got into the house.

'You will remember the kitchen window, broken and forced, things knocked over by the kitchen sink, clear signs that someone had climbed in that way. But none of Mr Stoker's fingerprints! Many of the Major's fingerprints, of course – that was to be expected, in his kitchen. But what is suggested here? That Mr Stoker wore gloves? No gloves were found on him or anywhere near the scene of the crime. And remember, he was taken straight from the library floor to hospital. Do you think he climbed in through the kitchen window and then carefully wiped all the surfaces on which he might have left his prints? Can you picture that happening, Members of the Jury? Is it within the realms of probability? Let us take this matter a little further. There were none of Mr Stoker's prints by the front door, none on the bell push, none at all. Does that, or does it not, Members of the Jury, support the suggestion that the Major heard Mr Stoker's car arrive and park at the back of the house, so he opened the front door to him? Was Mr Stoker a visitor the Major was expecting? Could it be, could it just possibly be, he was a visitor the Major had invited? The Major has said he never saw Mr Stoker before in his life. Can you really believe that, if he opened the door before Mr Stoker had even rung the bell? Let us see, shall we, if we can find the facts that might account for this.

'Mr Stoker undoubtedly visited Badgershide Wood on a number of occasions to see his girlfriend, Dawn Maresfield, who worked in the hairdresser's shop. He stayed with her in her flat which was in the town a few miles away, but you've heard that he sometimes drove her to work and picked her up again in his car. Now I have to give you a rather different picture of the lovable and eccentric Major. He was seriously sexually obsessed with Dawn, and you'll forgive me if I take up a little more of your time by reading an account of a conversation Miss Maresfield had with a highly reputable private detective, a Mr Ferdinand Ian Gilmour Newton.' (Here Fig Newton's evidence was read to the Jury.)

'What picture have you in your minds now, Members of the Jury, of Major Ben Dunkerton? Is it not of an old man sexually obsessed with a young woman almost to the point of insanity? So obsessed that he starts to give her the family jewellery, which she doesn't want, and writes her letters so embarrassingly obscene that she stops reading them. But does he get more and more deeply convinced that she might, at last, be tempted by his house and his wealth and agree to be his mistress, perhaps his wife? Only one thing, he was deluded enough to think, stood in his way. She has a lover, much younger and considerably more attractive than the elderly Major, and moreover a man with a criminal past whom she feels she can keep on the straight and narrow path of virtue. Does it need a great effort of your imagination, Members of the Jury, to understand how the Major managed to convince himself that, if only her lover was removed, Miss Dawn Maresfield might become available to him?

'How did he set about it? He had, we all have, read cases in the papers of householders shooting at intruders and earning public approval. Did this outrageous plan begin to form in the obsessed, in the by now mentally unbalanced, old man's mind? We all have to grow old, Members of the Jury, but we may hope to come to terms with the limitations of old age and not, in a vain effort to recover some of the joys of youth, commit desperate and criminal acts. So let us look again at the evidence and see if we can see behind the carefully calculated pretence and discover exactly what Major Ben Dunkerton did out of frustrated love and irrational jealousy.

'First he met Mr Stoker when he was walking in the woods. You may think that he had Mr Stoker under observation for some time and his plan to obliterate his rival had been carefully worked out. You'll remember he asked Mr Stoker about the attraction of Badgershide Wood, a question which might well have had a reference to the charms of Dawn. He then invented a story about a famous film director wanting to meet Mr Stoker, a ploy which had no point except to lure my client to the Major's house after ten-thirty on a particular night. He risked this pack of lies because he didn't expect David to live to tell the tale.

'What did the Major do on the night of the visit, Members of the Jury? Consider this as a possibility with me. Did he break his kitchen window? Did he, carefully and deliberately, create evidence of a break-in? Then, when he heard the car, did he open his front door and welcome in the man he was prepared to kill?

'It all went quite easily. He took Mr Stoker into the library, and showed him the old army pistol he had brought home from the war and never bothered to get a licence for. He told Mr Stoker to handle the weapon, so his fingerprints might be left on it. And then, Members of the Jury, he left the room to fetch his shotgun.

'None of us can know, not one of us should ever know, what it feels like to commit a murder. Was the Major afraid, or triumphant, or filled with nervous excitement? What it was that caused his shotgun to go off too soon we shall never know. Did his old finger press the trigger before he'd taken aim? Did he see Mr Stoker duck down behind the table and try to follow him like a moving bird? All we know is that he shot his rival for Dawn's affection, but, happily, he didn't kill him. His victim is here, in the bed beside me, still alive to tell you his story.

'Did this happen, Members of the Jury? Is that an account which fits all the facts of this case? If you think it's true you will, of course, acquit. But if you only think it might very well be true, if as a thoughtful and fair-minded Jury you cannot reject the possibility, then you must also acquit because the prosecution won't have satisfied you beyond reasonable doubt.

'Members of the Jury, this case has only occupied a short part of your lives. Perhaps an hour of late-night entertainment to take the place of the telly or the headphones. You will soon forget all about Badgershide Wood, and Snippers hair-dresser's, and the conversation in the Pizza Palace. But for David Stoker, whom I represent, this case represents the whole of his life. Is he to go free, or is he to be forced, by the devilish plot of a mad old man, back to his misspent younger life of prison and crime? It is his life I now leave, Members of the Jury, in your hands, confident that he will hear from you, in the fullness of time, those blessed words "Not guilty" which, more effectively than any surgery, will give life back to David Stoker.'

Then with a great flood of relief, I lay back on the pillows and closed my eyes. My final speech was over and I could do no more. The decision now had to be taken by other beds. It was the best moment of an anxious trial. As I lay resting, I heard the sound of distant voices. Verdicts came from the snorer, the tooth-grinder and many others. 'Not guilty,' they said, and 'Not guilty' they all voted. Even Ted the screw at the end of the chain piped up with 'I don't reckon David did it.' So the trial in the Princess Margaret ward was over.

Would I ever do the case down the Bailey? Would I ever repeat that closing speech to a real Jury, up and dressed, in a real Jury box? I felt sleep drifting over me, dulling my senses and darkening my world. Should I ever . . . Who knows? For the moment all I can say is, 'The defence rests.'